Flawless

by

Jana Richards

Flawless

Cover Art by *Nicola Martinez*

The Wild Rose Press
PO Box 706
Adams Basin, NY 14410-0706
Visit us at www.thewildrosepress.com

Publishing History
First Vintage Rose Edition, 2011
Print ISBN 978-1-5092-0449-6
Digital ISBN 978-1-62830-405-3

Published in the United States of America

Dedication

To my critique partner and friend Janet,
whose skills and encouragement
have made me a better writer.

"I said in the letter that you had not worked
as a gardener before, so he is not expecting you to know the difference between a delphinium and a dianthus." Monsieur Gagnon poured milk onto his porridge. "But he is expecting you to work hard. If you don't, you could be fired, or your cover could be blown."

"I can manage."

"The job might require a little more than sticking a shovel in the ground occasionally and spreading a bit of manure," Madeleine said. The others turned to stare at her.

She immediately regretted her sarcastic remark, regretted throwing his words in his face. She shouldn't let this man get to her, but she couldn't seem to stop herself. They needed to work together for the sake of the mission. But she hated him. After what he'd done to Jean Philippe…

Hunter's gaze locked with hers, and the heat of his anger scorched her clear across the room. She refused to back down from the challenge in his stare. She'd be damned if she'd let him intimidate her.

"Madeleine, enough." Monsieur Gagnon spoke sharply. "Regardless of your feelings, we need him. He is our only hope for getting the diamond out of the hands of the Nazis."

He was right. If they couldn't steal *le Coeur Bleu*, Jean Philippe would have died for nothing. She couldn't let that happen.

She inhaled deeply and looked away. "All right. We'll work together."

Chapter One

Down the hall, the heavy iron door creaked open, then closed again with a clang. Footsteps echoed on the stone floor, growing louder as they approached his prison room. When the footsteps suddenly stopped, Hunter Smith opened his eyes, surprised. In the eighteen months he'd been in this godforsaken place, no one had visited him, not his so-called friends, and certainly not his parents.

He turned his head. A neat little man in an impeccable black suit and bowler hat waited patiently for the guard to unlock the barred gate of his cell.

"He shouldn't give you any trouble, Guv'nor," the guard said as he opened the grate. "Not like some is in 'ere. Quick to steal your purse and slit yer throat for yer trouble, most of 'em. But I'll stay close by, just in case."

"That won't be necessary." The little man's voice reflected British public schools and a cultured upbringing. Hunter hated him immediately. "Please wait behind the outer door. I'll call you when I'm ready."

"If that's what you want, Guv'nor." The guard shrugged, relocked Hunter's cell, and retreated beyond the iron door with a clanking of keys. When the door had banged shut behind him, the little man spoke again.

"I have a proposition for you."

Hunter sat up, wincing as his feet touched the floor and his back protested in pain. The lumpy, too-short cot caused him no end of aggravation. "Is that so?"

"I want you to steal a diamond for me."

1

Hunter couldn't restrain a burst of mocking laughter. The irony of the little man's request would be funny if it weren't so pathetic.

"You want me to steal a diamond?" He rose and swept an arm around to encompass his prison cell. "I'd love to accommodate you, sir, but I'm afraid I'm a bit indisposed at the moment."

The little man surveyed the room, wrinkling his nose in distaste as his gaze met the bucket in the corner that served as Hunter's toilet. "If you agree to my request, I can have you released."

Hunter's heart rate tripled, but he kept his face neutral. He'd do almost anything to get out of this hell hole. Anything but steal another diamond.

He resumed his prone position on the cot. "I'm sorry you've wasted your time in coming here. I've turned over a new leaf. Seen the error of my ways." He flung one arm over his eyes. "Besides, I'm a lousy thief. That's how I ended up in here. I'm no longer interested in stealing jewels."

"I'm sorry to hear that."

Hunter waited to hear the man call for the guard, waited for the footsteps that would signal he had left the cell, but all remained silent. He lifted his arm and opened his eyes. The little man stood patiently, waiting. Hunter rose to his feet once more.

"Who the hell are you?"

"Allow me to introduce myself. My name is Alastair Campbell, and I am the head of the Special Operations Executive."

"Bully for you." Hunter had no idea what the Special Operations Executive was, but despite himself he was intrigued.

Campbell read his mind. "The SOE sends operatives to France, where they make contact with the French Resistance. We supply the Resistance with arms and two-way radios. The information they've supplied us on the movements of the Nazis in occupied France has been invaluable."

"Perhaps if I were British I might be interested in joining your little band of merry men. But I'm not British, and I'm not interested."

Arms folded, Hunter stared down at Campbell. His best efforts to intimidate the much smaller man were having little effect. Campbell smiled indulgently, like a kindly headmaster at a stubborn and not-very-bright student.

"I'm well aware of your American citizenship. I'm also aware that you've spent a good portion of your life living in France and that you speak perfect French."

That he'd lived in France wasn't exactly a secret, but the idea that someone had gone to the trouble to find out unsettled Hunter. What else did this little man know about him?

"Dropping into occupied France to have tea with the Resistance doesn't exactly sound like a good career move. I hear the Nazis don't take kindly to spies. I'm afraid I'll have to decline your lovely offer." Again Hunter lay on his cot and closed his eyes, waiting for Campbell to leave.

"Not even for *le Coeur Bleu*?"

Hunter's eyes snapped open, his blood pounding in his ears. "What do you know about the Blue Heart?"

"Only that it is one of the most famous and rare diamonds in the world, over thirty carats, and said to be flawless."

Hunter rose from his cot and paced his small cell, heart racing. "Ah, finally something you don't know. *Le Coeur Bleu* has a small flaw, an inclusion visible only with a jeweler's loupe."

Campbell inclined his head. "My mistake. I bow to your superior knowledge of the stone."

He met Campbell's calm stare. He doubted this man ever made mistakes. "What else do you know about the diamond?"

"I know the diamond is reputed to have magical

powers. Some even say it is cursed."

"You don't really believe in magical powers, do you?" Hunter scoffed.

Campbell lifted one shoulder in a delicate shrug. "Perhaps, perhaps not. Do you think your friend Jean Philippe Bertrand believed in magic?"

All the air rushed out of Hunter's lungs and he struggled to breathe. "What do you know about Jean Philippe?"

"That he came into possession of *le Coeur Bleu* and was murdered for it by the Nazis."

Hunter dropped heavily onto his cot, shock and pain turning his knees to water. Snippets of the telegram he'd received from his best friend a few weeks before his arrest flashed in his head. *Need to buy Heartstone times two from Jewish refugee. Desperate. Send cash.* Hunter had immediately wired JP the money to buy the Heartstone, the name by which *le Coeur Bleu* was sometimes known. He never heard from Jean Philippe again. In all the months of his captivity he'd clung to the hope that Jean Philippe was safe. But now that hope was dashed.

"Dead? You're sure?"

"Yes. The SOE is very well connected in France. I can assure you, your friend was killed for *le Coeur Bleu.*"

Guilt flowed through Hunter's veins like a poison. If he hadn't sent the money, JP wouldn't have had the diamond and the Nazis would have had no reason to kill him.

Campbell stepped closer to Hunter's cot, determination glittering in his eyes. "I'm giving you the opportunity to avenge your friend's death. Will you take it, Mr. Smith?"

Anger filled Hunter, making him pace his cell once more. How dare this man use JP's death for his own purposes? "How is stealing the Blue Heart going to avenge Jean Philippe's death? It's just a stone, Mr. Campbell. Very pretty, very valuable, but just a rock. Is stealing it going to bring him back?"

"No, it won't," Campbell conceded, "but it will hurt the Nazis immensely. I can assure you that taking *le Coeur Bleu* from them will reduce their capacity to fight, Mr. Smith. It may even shorten the war and provide the turning point we're looking for. Is this not what your friend would have wanted?"

As Hunter stared into Campbell's round face, he remembered the last stinging conversation he'd had with his friend. *"If you used your God-given talents for good instead of squandering them on party tricks, perhaps you'd be a lot happier. It's time to grow up, Hunter. For once in your life, be a man."*

Perhaps the time had finally come.

"How soon can I get out of here?"

Campbell smiled in satisfaction. "Follow me."

****

The full moon lit the night sky, showing the way. When the co-pilot turned in his seat and grinned at Hunter, he looked more like a boy on an adventure than a soldier on a deadly serious spy mission.

"This is where it gets interesting," he said. "We're now over occupied France. We should be at the rendezvous point in approximately ten minutes."

Hunter nodded and stared out the window of the rear cockpit to the land below. Not a single light burned in the French countryside, giving the eerie impression of abandonment, as if everyone had fled. Or been killed.

He shook off the disturbing sensation. He knew that somewhere down there his French contacts waited for him and for the load of arms and ammunition accompanying him. The plane itself had made several of these excursions into occupied France to pick up or drop off operatives and bring much-needed supplies to the Resistance. The sturdy little Lysander had the advantage of being able to land and take off on short, makeshift runways and could fly low enough to be invisible to radar. The perfect spy plane.

The pilots consulted their maps and compasses, their only navigational aids aside from the full moon. Suddenly, the co-pilot pointed toward the ground below.

"There's the spot. Prepare for landing."

Hunter peered out the window once more. Four lights flickered beneath them, marking a crude landing strip. The plane circled once before making a bone-jarring landing on what must have been a farmer's field.

As the plane came to a stop, a car skidded to a halt beside them and three people jumped out. Hunter had been prepared for the landing by the SOE at his three-week training session. He grabbed his knapsack and the suitcase-sized two-way radio he was delivering and opened the rear cockpit door, descending as quickly as he could down the ladder that had been fixed to the port side of the plane for quick entries and escapes.

Two men unloaded rifles from the large tank under the belly. Another person retrieved and extinguished the torches used to light the runway for the landing. In a matter of a few minutes the arms were loaded in the trunk of the car and the Lysander began its taxi down the field, picking up speed until it lifted off the ground. Within seconds, the plane disappeared into the night sky, its black matte finish making it all but invisible.

"*Dépêchez-vous*! Get in the car!"

Hunter tossed his gear into the back seat behind the front passenger. The rest of the crew piled in, and the driver took off, tires spinning.

No one spoke as they raced away. Everyone knew the danger. Though the Lysander might be invisible to radar, the Germans would have heard its approach and were likely searching for them right now. If they were caught by a German patrol with arms stowed in the trunk, it was all over.

A few moments later the car came to a screeching halt, dust flying all around it. The driver turned to Hunter.

"Get out! Quickly!"

They hadn't mentioned this in the three-week training course.

When he hesitated, the driver shouted again. "Get out!"

Hunter grabbed the radio and his knapsack and wrenched open the car door, stumbling in his haste to get out. As soon as he slammed the door shut, the car took off again, pebbles and dirt flying. He shielded his eyes from the onslaught. What the hell was he supposed to do now?

When the dust cleared, he realized he wasn't alone. Someone stood just down the road, waiting. Hunter could only hope this was part of the plan, that this person was friend rather than foe. He straightened his shoulders, picked up the radio, and moved forward.

For a long moment the person stood watching him, saying nothing. In frustration, Hunter broke the silence.

"Hello? Can you help me?" he said in French.

"Monsieur Smith?"

Hunter hesitated, surprised. A woman's voice. He hadn't expected his contact to be a woman.

"*Oui.*"

It had been a while since he'd spoken French. Hell, when he'd been in prison he'd barely spoken at all. The words still felt rusty on his tongue, but the French of his childhood, his childhood with Jean Philippe, was coming back to him quickly.

"We must get back to town before the sun comes up," the woman said as she started briskly down a dirt path off the main road, not waiting for him. Hunter hoisted his knapsack onto his back and picked up the radio, hurrying to catch up with her.

"You know my name, but I don't know yours."

"It's Madeleine."

"Where are you taking me?"

"To Lille. It is about five kilometers from here. You will stay with Monsieur Gagnon until he finds you another place to stay. You came here to look for work. You will

7

present yourself at Chateau de Maisoneuve tomorrow as a gardener. The Germans are always looking for someone to do their dirty work for them."

Her words came out clipped, as if she were annoyed with him for not knowing all the details of his cover already. Her attitude irritated him.

"Look, Madeleine, in their infinite wisdom, Special Operations Executive didn't bother to tell me anything about my cover, so don't blame me."

"What exactly do you know about being a gardener?" She picked up her pace, and Hunter had to lengthen his stride to keep up with her.

"What's to know? I stick a shovel into the ground occasionally and spread manure. It's just a cover. I'm here for *le Coeur Bleu*, not the roses."

Madeleine threw up her hands. "Ah, yes, *le Coeur Bleu*. That's all you're really interested in, isn't it?"

"Of course I'm interested in it. Getting it away from the Germans is the whole reason I'm here."

"You mean stealing it."

What was her problem? "Yes, I mean stealing it. You don't think the Nazis are going to hand it over if I say 'pretty please,' do you?"

Madeleine stopped suddenly and spun to face him. The sky had lightened just enough for him to see the fury in her eyes. "You're nothing but a common thief. I know all about you, Monsieur Smith. I know you were imprisoned for jewel theft in London. I know the only reason you got out was because Monsieur Campbell needed you to steal this jewel. You think it is better to steal *le Coeur Bleu* than to rot in jail. Do you think this is a lark, a game we play here, Monsieur Smith? I can assure you, you will soon regret coming to France."

She turned on her heel and marched off, leaving Hunter to stare at her retreating back, angry and dumbfounded at her holier-than-thou attitude. He stalked after her once more.

"I can assure *you*, mademoiselle, I already regret coming to France."

Chapter Two

"From now on you will be known as Jacques Lemay, Monsieur Smith."

Monsieur Gagnon filled his pipe, dropping bits of tobacco onto his wife's immaculate floor. Madeleine sat off to one side of Monsieur Gagnon's kitchen, watching as Madame Gagnon prepared breakfast for her husband and their "guest." Madeleine silently seethed as Smith—*non,* Lemay—helped himself to another piece of bread. Did he have to eat so much? Didn't he know that food was scarce here in Lille, just as it was all over France?

She listened as Smith handed over the new two-way radio to Monsieur Gagnon and explained its use.

"It's supposed to have a clearer and stronger signal than the radio you're using now," Smith said. He flipped a few dials to illustrate. "They also told me it is easier to scramble the signal to avoid detection."

"*Bon.*" Monsieur Gagnon beamed in pleasure. "Good communications are essential to our work. Thank you for bringing it."

"No problem. What else can you tell me about my cover here?"

"You are to work as a junior gardener at the chateau. I wrote to the head gardener, as if I was you, inquiring about work. He's desperate for help. The Germans have rounded up many young Frenchmen and shipped them east to work in factories in Germany, so there are few able-bodied men available. You start tomorrow."

He paused as his wife set a bowl of porridge in front of him. Monsieur Gagnon could not be connected with Jacques

Lemay in any way; their comings and goings to this house had to be done with the utmost discretion. Madeleine knew the importance of keeping Monsieur Gagnon and his wife safe. He was the heart of their operation, their connection to the outside world through the radio he operated. If something went wrong and Hunter Smith was captured, it was crucial that no trails led back to Monsieur Gagnon. The safety of their *réseaux*, their Resistance network, depended on it. She hoped Smith understood the danger.

"I said in the letter that you had not worked as a gardener before, so he is not expecting you to know the difference between a delphinium and a dianthus." Monsieur Gagnon poured milk onto his porridge. "But he is expecting you to work hard. If you don't, you could be fired, or your cover could be blown."

"I can manage."

"The job might require a little more than sticking a shovel in the ground occasionally and spreading a bit of manure," Madeleine said. The others turned to stare at her.

She immediately regretted her sarcastic remark, regretted throwing his words in his face. She shouldn't let this man get to her, but she couldn't seem to stop herself. They needed to work together for the sake of the mission. But she hated him. After what he'd done to Jean Philippe…

Hunter's gaze locked with hers, and the heat of his anger scorched her clear across the room. She refused to back down from the challenge in his stare. She'd be damned if she'd let him intimidate her.

"Madeleine, enough." Monsieur Gagnon spoke sharply. "Regardless of your feelings, we need him. He is our only hope for getting the diamond out of the hands of the Nazis."

He was right. If they couldn't steal *le Coeur Bleu*, Jean Philippe would have died for nothing. She couldn't let that happen.

She inhaled deeply and looked away. "All right. We'll work together."

Monsieur Gagnon clapped his hands together. *"Bon.* After breakfast Madeleine and I will go to work while Monsieur Smith, *pardon,* Monsieur Lemay, rests. Tonight we will go over our plans."

"Do you work at the chateau?" Hunter asked.

"Oui. I work in the motor pool looking after the Germans' vehicles, and Madeleine is a housemaid inside the chateau. Her knowledge of the building will be invaluable to you, monsieur."

Her assignment since arriving in Lille two months ago had been to infiltrate the inside of the chateau. Both she and Collette had secured jobs working as housemaids. It was Collette who had learned of the general's plans for *le Coeur Bleu.* Madeleine's heart ached for the vibrant young woman she'd known for only a few weeks but had grown to care for like a sister.

For you too, Collette. I do this for you.

Would everyone she loved die before this damned war was over?

****

Madeleine applied beeswax to a soft cloth and polished the armoire until it glowed. A wonderful piece, probably eighteenth century, the armoire was made of beautifully grained mahogany with a rich chocolate-red patina. The brass pulls and escutcheons appeared delicate but had stood the test of time for nearly two hundred years. As she polished the fine wood, Madeleine wondered about the armoire's history. Who had built such a fine piece? Who had owned it over the years? Who had the Germans stolen it from?

The chateau itself had been owned by the Baroness de Maisoneuve, whose husband's family had lived in the chateau for generations. After her husband's death the chateau had fallen into a state of genteel disrepair. Childless, elderly, and somewhat frail, the baroness had neither the strength nor the financial resources to properly maintain the old castle. She'd been forced to sell her best pieces of furniture to buy food and to heat the place in winter. When the Germans invaded France and took over Lille, General Klaus Dietrich had expropriated the chateau as his headquarters and living accommodation, and taken over this grand master suite for himself, furnishing it with the best pieces. The baroness had been moved to a small cottage on the estate but was otherwise unharmed. People from the town took turns bringing her food and looking after her needs.

Ever since General Dietrich had taken over the chateau there had been regular deliveries of fine pieces of furniture such as the armoire, as well as paintings, silver serving dishes and candlesticks, beautiful porcelain dishes, and exquisite decorative ceramics. Where was it all coming from?

The rumor circulating through the Resistance was that much of the loot came from the houses of wealthy French Jews deported to the east. A shiver of unease rippled through Madeleine. Where were those families now?

Madeleine finished her work and stepped from the low stool that had allowed her to reach the top of the armoire. After one last admiring glance at her handiwork, she picked up her supplies and prepared to move into the next bedroom to polish the furniture there. As she turned to leave, the door opened and General Dietrich swept into the room. Madeleine's stomach lurched in apprehension. Since Collette's death the general had been watching her, preparing, she supposed, to make her his next mistress. She had been careful not to be on her own with him, to make sure she was always in a group. But now here she was, alone with the general in his own bedroom. Madeleine cursed herself for her carelessness. She never should have come into his bedroom unaccompanied while he was in the chateau.

A slow smile spread across the general's face when he

saw her. "Your name is Madeleine, is it not?" he asked in very good French. The intelligence on the general said that his mother was French and that he had attended university at the Sorbonne in Paris in the late 1920s. He needn't have bothered speaking French, since Madeleine understood German very well. It was one of the reasons she'd been assigned to the chateau.

But the general didn't need to know that.

"*Oui,* monsieur." Madeleine glanced at the door and contemplated making a run for it. Unfortunately, the general stood between her and escape.

He chuckled when he saw the direction of her glance. "Come, come, *ma petite.* Stay a while. Surely you don't find being alone with me so distasteful." He closed the distance between them and ran his finger gently over Madeleine's cheek. She restrained herself from slapping him hard across the face.

"We should get to know each other better, more intimately." He snaked his arm around her waist and crushed her against him. Madeleine resisted, dropping her cleaning supplies and using both hands on his chest to push him away so she could take several steps from him.

"Sir, I am a married woman!"

She held up her left hand, displaying her mother's gold wedding band. She had begun wearing the ring as a talisman against evil in the last two years. Many young French girls had been raped or coerced into liaisons with German soldiers in exchange for food or other favors. Up until now the ring had served as a deterrent to most men.

The general, however, was not most men. He laughed, unperturbed by her fictional married status.

"Where is this husband? I don't see him here."

Madeleine knew from Collette that the general considered himself, in his mid-forties, to be an attractive man. Given his tall, lean physique, thick blond, wavy hair and icy blue eyes, many women would agree. But Madeleine looked at the general and saw only ugliness. She knew what he was capable of. He'd killed Jean Philippe.

And Collette. It sickened her to be in the same room as Dietrich.

"My husband is away in Paris, working," she said. "He'll be home very soon."

The general approached her once more. Madeleine retreated until her back was against the armoire and she had no place left to go. He pulled her against him and lowered his face to hers.

"I don't mind sharing you. And I'm sure he won't mind either, if he knows what's good for him."

He kissed her, a hard, punishing kiss meant to control and possess. Madeleine tried at first to resist, but he was far too strong. When his tongue ravished her mouth and he tugged at her clothes, she resigned herself to her fate. She made her mind go far away, to better times. To Jean Philippe.

An insistent knock sounded at the door. "General!" a German voice called. "You are needed urgently in the ballroom!"

With a curse the general pushed himself away from Madeleine and straightened his uniform.

"We will meet again, *ma petite*."

He marched to the door and left the room without a backward glance. Madeleine sagged in relief against the armoire, tears trickling down her face. As she rebuttoned her blouse and tucked it back into her skirt, she wondered how she could evade the general now that he'd decided she was his. As much as she despised the thought, despised him, she knew she'd likely have to play the part of his mistress, at least until the mission was over.

****

Hunter slept most of the day in Madame Gagnon's spare room, waking in the late afternoon to the enticing smells of fresh bread baking. He followed his nose into the

15

kitchen, where Monsieur Gagnon was sitting at the table with a glass of wine.

"Ah, there you are, monsieur." He poured Hunter a glass of wine and handed it to him. "I trust you slept well."

"Yes, very well. Thank you."

"*Bon.* When Madeleine arrives, we will eat. Then we will go over our plans."

Hunter nodded, but privately he worried about Madeleine's obvious dislike for him. She'd made it abundantly clear she thought he was nothing but a thief and a scoundrel. How could they work together when she didn't trust him? How could he trust her?

When Madeleine arrived a short time later, they all sat down to dinner. Her clear porcelain skin looked even paler than it had last night, her demeanor far more subdued. Her blue eyes held a haunted quality that hadn't been there the previous evening.

Monsieur Gagnon noticed, as well. "What's happened?" he asked as he filled her wine glass.

She looked down at her plate, not meeting Monsieur Gagnon's pointed gaze. She pushed around the pieces of beef and carrot in Madame Gagnon's excellent stew.

"Nothing I can't handle."

"Madeleine."

Monsieur Gagnon's sharp rebuke had them all staring at him. Madeleine lifted her gaze to his.

"Tell me what's happened."

The command was spoken with both authority and kindness. Hunter saw Madeleine swallow. A tiny shudder shook her delicate shoulders.

"The general made…advances on me today."

Madame Gagnon gasped and took Madeleine's hand. She clung to the older woman.

"What happened, exactly?" Monsieur Gagnon asked. When Madeleine hesitated, he added gently, "I'm sorry, but you have to tell us. We need to know what we're facing."

She nodded and briefly closed her eyes. When she opened them again, her expression was calm and filled with determination. "Yes, I know."

She told them of the general's attempted rape. Hunter's blood ran cold.

When she finished, Monsieur Gagnon nodded. "I am truly sorry, Madeleine. All I can tell you is to avoid the general as much as you can for the next week."

She nodded, but Hunter could see that was little comfort. How could she avoid the man when he was determined to seek her out?

Madame Gagnon put her arm around Madeleine's shoulders. "There must be some way we can protect her. We can't let what happened to Collette happen to Madeleine, too."

Hunter was almost afraid to know. "What happened to Collette?"

Madeleine turned her face away, and Madame Gagnon embraced her once more.

"She was killed by General Dietrich," Monsieur Gagnon said in a flat voice. "The general made her his mistress, in much the same way he is trying to do with Madeleine. She was a beautiful, gentle girl, but she was brave, as well. He found her rifling through his papers in his office, and he executed her himself, in front of the entire staff."

Madeleine clung to Madame Gagnon as the older woman quietly wept.

"But before she died she brought us information of *le Coeur Bleu* and the general's plans for it," Madeleine said. "We owe it to Collette to make sure the Nazis fail. I will not run away."

Her words were spoken with quiet determination. Madeleine's courage awed Hunter. Despite the risks to herself, she was willing to do whatever it took to disrupt the Nazis' plans. He wondered if he would be as brave.

Monsieur Gagnon cleared his throat. "Come now. Let us finish the delicious dinner my good wife has prepared for us. Then we will talk."

They ate the rest of their meal in silence. When everyone had finished, Madame Gagnon cleared the table and her husband produced a bottle of brandy and three glasses. He poured a small measure in each glass, passed two of them to Hunter and Madeleine, and then lifted his own glass in a toast.

"To the mission."

"To Collette," Madeleine added.

They downed the brandy in one gulp. Monsieur Gagnon set his glass on the table and wiped his mouth with the back of his hand. "Now it is time to go to work. What have you been told so far, Monsieur Lemay?"

"Almost nothing. All Mr. Campbell told me was that stealing *le Coeur Bleu* was important to the Allies and could be a turning point in the war."

"That was wise. It is best not to know too much. Had you been captured, you could tell little to the Gestapo, even if they tortured you."

Hunter nodded grimly. "Lucky for me I made it here undetected. So what's the story of the Blue Heart?"

"General Dietrich came into possession of *le Coeur Bleu* almost two years ago. He's kept the fact that the diamond is hidden away in the Chateau de Maisoneuve a secret. If his higher-ups in Berlin had discovered he had the stone, they would have snatched it away from him, depriving him of the glory of being the savior of the Third Reich."

"The savior of the Third Reich?"

Monsieur Gagnon paused as he stuffed tobacco into his pipe and lit it. "*Le Coeur Bleu* is valuable only if it can be traded for something desperately needed. The Nazis must trade the diamond for what they need the most. Can you guess what that is, Monsieur Lemay?"

"I guess that would be equipment to make war.

Airplanes, submarines, tanks."

"Very good. And what does all of this equipment need to run?"

"They need fuel. Gasoline and oil."

"*Oui, absolument.*" Monsieur Gagnon pointed his pipe at Hunter. "Without fuel, none of this machinery of war can operate. But the Nazis have a problem. There are no oil fields in Germany. Right now most of their fuel needs are supplied by the oil fields they confiscated in Romania. But if they are to win the war they need much more than those oil fields can supply."

"Most of the oil for the Allied war effort comes from America, doesn't it?" Hunter asked.

"Yes," agreed Monsieur Gagnon, "so of course the Nazis have no access to it. There are oil fields in the Middle East, particularly in Persia, but they supply only a small amount of oil. In any event, that region is controlled by the British. So that means the Nazis have to come up with a new solution for their fuel needs."

"So what is that?"

"Synthetic oil," Madeleine chimed in. "Germany may not have oil fields, but they do have vast supplies of coal. Germans have been making oil from coal for several years."

"They want to build more synthetic oil plants, but they lack the materials to build them," Monsieur Gagnon added. "Massive amounts of steel are required, which they don't have and no one will sell to them."

"Until now. It's taken Dietrich these past two years to find just the right buyer for the diamond." Madeleine opened a small briefcase and took out a photograph. She set it in front of Hunter. "This is Karlheinz Schmidt. He's a South African businessman who has made his fortune in mining, particularly the mining of diamonds and iron ore."

Hunter studied the picture of Schmidt. The man appeared exceedingly ordinary, like someone he might meet on the streets of London, New York, or Peoria, Illinois.

"Isn't South Africa allied with Britain and the United States?" Hunter asked.

"Yes, officially South Africa is part of the Allies, but many South Africans of German descent are sympathetic to Germany or, as in Schmidt's case, to the Nazi regime."

"Schmidt considers himself a connoisseur of diamonds," Madeleine continued. "He's wanted to get his hands on *le Coeur Bleu* for years. He's willing to trade several tons of iron ore and steel for it. We can't let that happen."

"And that's where I come in," Hunter said. "I break into the chateau and open the safe where the diamond is kept. Then what do we do with it?"

"We have to get it out of the country," Monsieur Gagnon said. "We can't let the Nazis have another chance to get their hands on it. We'll arrange a plane to pick you up and fly you back to England as soon as the diamond is in our hands."

"But we don't have much time," Madeleine added. "According to the information Collette gathered, Schmidt will arrive in Lille a week from today to examine the stone for authenticity. If he is satisfied, he will give the word for his ships to leave South Africa. They will be escorted by German submarines up the west coast of Africa, through the straits of Gibraltar, and into the Mediterranean. The ships will dock in Italy and the materials brought by train to Germany."

"And if we don't succeed in stealing the diamond and getting it out of France?" Hunter asked. "What happens then? Do we have a Plan B?"

"If we fail, the Allies will try to bomb the ships. But bombing the ships of an Allied country could pit the Allies against each other. That's assuming the Allies can mount such an air attack. The British Air Force was severely damaged in the Battle of Britain and they're just now rebuilding. The Americans entered the war only a few months ago. No, we cannot fail, Monsieur Lemay."

"Besides," Madeleine added with a pointed look at Hunter, "if we fail, that likely means we will all be dead. I, for one, would like to avoid that situation."

Hunter grinned despite the seriousness of her words. He could almost hear Jean Philippe telling him in that intense way he'd had that failure was not an option. JP would want him to finish what he started.

"At least on that, mademoiselle, we can agree."

Chapter Three

Madeleine lifted her face to the noonday sun, grateful for the warmth and the short respite from her work in the chateau. Since the spring day was so glorious, she'd decided to take her lunch outside in the gardens. Besides, the general was home today, and she wanted to stay as far away from him as she could.

She sat on an old stone bench beside the reflecting pool and the newly refurbished fountain and listened to the murmuring water and the birds singing in the trees. Madeleine sighed and took a bite of the sandwich the cook had prepared for her. It was so peaceful here. How hard it was to believe that not far away a war raged, and inside the walls of the chateau the general and his men plotted the destruction of her country and the subjugation of her people.

She couldn't let that happen. She was no hero, and she certainly didn't want to die, but doing her small part to fight the Nazis was worth giving up her life.

She hoped it wouldn't come to that.

But then she thought of Collette and Jean Philippe and knew dying was a distinct possibility.

The birds suddenly took to the sky, their cries calling a warning as General Dietrich strode between the trees lining the entrance to the fountain area, his boots gleaming in the sunshine. The self-satisfied look on his face told Madeleine he did not mean for her to get away this time.

Madeleine quickly rose and glanced around for something to use as a weapon. There was nothing, not even a rock or a stick. The general's gardeners had groomed the property to perfection. She lifted her chin in a show of bravado.

"I must get back to work."

He grabbed her arm as she tried to pass. "They are not expecting you for...a while. The cook told me you were here."

Madeleine silently cursed the older woman, but then cursed herself instead. The cook was terrified of the general. Madeleine should have known better than to tell her she planned to take her lunch here.

He pulled her against him, one arm holding her in a vise-like grip. "I would have preferred our first time together in my bed, with silk sheets and soft music playing. But this will do quite nicely."

He kissed her hard, forcing her mouth open to accept his probing tongue. His free hand, large and calloused, found the hem of her skirt and snaked up her thigh. He tugged at her panties, inching them downward. For a moment Madeleine thought she would be sick, but then she made her mind go blank. This wasn't happening to her. This was a bad dream, and soon she would wake up in Jean Philippe's arms.

Jean Philippe! Please help me!

"Madeleine!"

The angry male voice surprised her. Dietrich released his hold just enough to allow Madeleine to free herself and run toward the exit, her eyes blurred with tears. A strong hand grabbed her arm and, for the second time, she was prevented from leaving the fountain glade.

"Slut!"

Madeleine's head snapped back from the force of the slap across her face. Her head swam for a moment, but when her vision cleared she looked up into the face of the American.

Damn him! The bastard! What did he think he was doing?

She roared in indignation and raised her hand to slap him back. He easily intercepted her blow, holding both her arms behind her back with his as he brought her tight against his body.

"Is this how you greet your husband? Have I been away so long that you turn to someone else?"

Her husband?

Madeleine barely had time to process this bit of news before Hunter's mouth descended on hers. She braced herself for a hard, punishing kiss much like the general's. But instead Hunter's kiss was gentle, soft, almost...pleasant.

He released her arms and somehow they wound themselves around his neck. At last his lips left hers, and he kissed her cheek.

"I'm sorry," he whispered in her ear.

Madeleine stared up into his face, not knowing what to say or do. She wasn't even sure what to feel.

"Well, this is a touching scene. The prodigal husband returns." The general straightened his uniform as he approached them, his eyes blazing with anger. Madeleine shrank against Hunter's side, his strong arm around her, holding her up.

"Yes," Hunter said. "I just arrived this morning from Paris to start my new job here at the chateau as a gardener. We couldn't bear being apart any longer."

When he looked into her face, Madeleine could almost believe he meant what he said. His eyes were full of tenderness and his smile spoke of deep fondness, love even. Her mind whirled in confusion, but she managed to return his smile. They both had parts to play.

The general laid a possessive hand on her shoulder. "Your wife and I were just getting acquainted. In future I do not wish to be interrupted."

Hunter's hand tightened on her waist. "You will not touch my wife again."

The general's lip turned up in a sneer. "If you wish to continue working at the chateau, if you wish to continue living in Lille, you will not interfere."

Madeleine's blood turned to ice. Surely, the American would not be so stupid as to antagonize the general! The man was capable of murder. This she knew for a fact.

"Jacques, please. Don't."

The general laughed, pleased with himself. "Listen to your wife, monsieur. She knows what is good for both of you."

"I am concerned for my wife, monsieur." The thrust of Hunter's chin told Madeleine he refused to be intimidated. She inwardly groaned. He was going to get them both killed. "The last time we were together she was very ill. She is pregnant with my child."

Both Madeleine and the general stared at him. She did her best to hide her shock. Hunter gently smoothed her hair from her forehead.

"How are you feeling, *ma petite*? Are you still ill every morning?"

She blinked at him a moment. "*Oui*, very ill. Every morning."

Hunter took her face in both his hands and kissed her forehead. "Now that I'm here, I'll look after you."

General Dietrich dropped his hand from her shoulder. "You're pregnant?"

She turned to face him, hoping he couldn't see the lie in her eyes. "Yes."

He glanced at her belly and then at her face, his expression full of disgust. Without a word he marched back to the chateau, his steps brisk and his spine rigid with anger. They watched until he disappeared inside the chateau. Only then did Madeleine release the breath she was holding.

"Are you all right?"

The concern in his voice undid her. She put her hand over her mouth to stop the tears, but still they came, great shuddering sobs that buckled her knees. Hunter pulled her close and held her, his touch offering support and understanding, and much-needed strength. It felt so good to be held once more, to be touched and comforted. She hadn't been held in so long, not since…

Not since Jean Philippe had been murdered.

What was she doing? Hunter had betrayed the man she'd loved, causing his death. The man she *still* loved.

She pulled away from him abruptly.

"We'll have to make it look good," he said.

"What are you talking about?"

He grinned at her. "Our marriage. The general won't believe we're married or that you're pregnant unless we look like a couple. We'll have to spend time together, do things that married people do, like kiss."

"Kiss?" The idea was both appalling and strangely exciting. "Don't be ridiculous. I'm sure that won't be—"

"Shh!"

Hunter pulled her into his arms, covering her mouth with his in a hard, insistent kiss. From the corner of her eye Madeleine saw a couple of housemaids approach the fountain. She struggled for a moment, her hands pushing against his chest, but then something changed. His kiss softened, sweetened, his hands gentling on her waist. Her hands slid up his broad, muscled chest to his shoulders. She reveled in the feel of his solidness, his strength. The feel of his silky hair at the nape of his neck was unexpected. So much of this man was hard, iron-like, that the silkiness of his dark, overlong hair came as a surprise.

One of the housemaids giggled, rousing Madeleine from her trance. She broke away from Hunter, confused. He was someone she should hate for what he'd done to Jean Philippe, yet he'd just saved her from being raped, maybe even saved her life.

And his kiss. How could she explain her reaction to his kiss?

When she glanced into Hunter's face, he looked as shocked as she felt. The thought that she wasn't the only one confused comforted her. She took Hunter's hand between the two of hers and turned to her co-workers with a smile.

"I want to introduce you to my husband, Jacques Lemay."

****

When their workday was done they met on the front steps of the chateau. Hunter held out his hand to her. Madeleine hesitated, staring at his hand. She was reluctant to touch him again, afraid of the emotions his touch had ignited earlier.

"People are watching, Madeleine," he said quietly with a smile. "They'll think you don't like your husband."

Her gaze locked with his. With a lift of her chin, she held out her hand. She might find his touch disconcerting, but she'd be damned if she let him or anyone else know it.

She gave him a brilliant smile. "We can't let them think that, can we?"

Neither of them said a word during the ten-minute walk to Monsieur Gagnon's house. Madeleine couldn't think properly with Hunter so close, and it annoyed her. What was wrong with her? He might have saved her, but she didn't like him. She had to focus on the mission and her part in it.

And she could never forget how he had betrayed Jean Philippe. The American could not be trusted.

Madeleine dropped Hunter's hand the minute they reached Monsieur Gagnon's house. They had circled, as if heading toward her cottage, then taken a side alley and made their way to the back entry of the house. After checking that no one had followed them and that no one watched them arrive, she knocked twice on the door before entering. Monsieur Gagnon was already home and seated at the table with a mug of something hot and steaming in front of him.

"Ah, there you are. I understand you two had a very eventful day."

"So you heard."

Gagnon nodded at Hunter. "I make it my business to know what is going on at the chateau. So what is this I hear about you two being married?"

Madeleine sighed and told him the story, editing the details of her near rape. "Do you think the Germans will believe we're married?"

"Only if the French staff believes it." He took a sip from his mug. "If the staff treats you as a married couple, the Germans will, too."

Madeleine sighed. "I suppose I can pretend to be in love with him while we are at the chateau."

"I'm sorry pretending to be in love with me is so distasteful to you."

Madeleine noted the angry set of Hunter's jaw. "I only meant, monsieur, that it is difficult to fake feelings that are not there."

"You seemed to like kissing me well enough."

"That's not true, you…you arrogant American!"

"Stop it, you two. Enough!"

Madame Gagnon slapped her wooden spoon against the table, her normally placid face flushed with anger. Madeleine and Hunter both stared at her in surprise, giving her their complete attention. Even Monsieur Gagnon raised his eyebrows.

"No one will believe you are a newly married couple with a baby on the way if you do nothing but bicker."

Monsieur Gagnon chuckled. "And no one will believe they are married if they do not bicker at all."

She pointed her wooden spoon at him. "This is not a joke, Jean. Do you not remember what happened to Collette? I do not want the same thing to happen to Madeleine."

The smile left Monsieur Gagnon's face. "You are right, of course, *ma chère*. What do you suggest?"

"It is not enough that they pretend to be married only at the chateau. People talk. If someone notices that Monsieur Lemay sleeps somewhere besides his wife's cottage, tongues will wag. There are many who would be happy to give this news to the general in exchange for some small benefit.

Until this mission is over, they need to live together as a married couple."

A cold ripple of apprehension crawled down Madeleine's spine. She knew the town was equally divided between sympathizers to the Resistance and German collaborators. But the idea that Hunter would invade her tiny personal space was unthinkable.

"Madame, surely that will not be necessary."

"It is only for a few days, until Monsieur Lemay and the diamond are safely in England."

Monsieur Gagnon frowned. "Now that everyone thinks Madeleine is married to Monsieur Lemay, it will seem strange if he suddenly leaves without her, especially if she is to have a baby."

"*Oui*, she will not be safe from the general, and he might even suspect her in the theft of the diamond. She will have to leave France with Monsieur Lemay."

"No!" Madeleine stared at them in shock. "I can't do that!"

"Madeleine, it won't be safe for you here once he steals the diamond."

"I won't go anywhere with him! I don't trust him!"

"What are you talking about?"

She pointed an accusing finger at Hunter, her hand shaking. She could no longer keep her rage and frustration locked inside her heart. "He killed my husband. He killed Jean Philippe."

Chapter Four

Hunter stared at her, dumbfounded. "You were married to Jean Philippe? Jean Philippe Bertrand?"

Tears streamed down Madeleine's face. Madame Gagnon put a supporting arm around her shoulders. "Yes."

"When? When were you married to him?"

"We met in Paris six months before the Germans invaded. We had only three months together as husband and wife."

Hunter pulled his hand through his hair. Why hadn't JP told him about Madeleine? He closed his eyes and shook his head.

"It doesn't make sense. He was my best friend. He would have told me if he'd married."

Madeleine's chin lifted in defiance, her eyes blazing. "You question our marriage? How dare you? Because of you, he is dead!"

"That's not true! I was in England. How could I have possibly done anything to hurt Jean Philippe?" Distrust and anger and grief whirled in his head. "Why should I believe you were married to him?"

"Because he gave me this!"

Madeleine bent her head and unclasped a gold necklace. She thrust it into Hunter's hand.

"Jean Philippe gave this to me on our wedding day. It belonged to his mother."

Hunter stared at the fine gold chain attached to a small locket engraved with the letters HB. Hélène Bertrand. He didn't have to open the locket to see the tiny pictures of Jean Philippe's parents on their wedding day, and the one of JP taken on the day they both graduated from private school. Hélène Bertrand had practically raised him along with her own son. His father the ambassador and his mother the socialite were too busy to bother.

"Jean Philippe's mother wore this locket every day. She was an amazing woman." He handed the necklace back to Madeleine.

"I never met her." She refastened the necklace and tucked the locket back inside her blouse. "She died before we met. I also have our marriage license. It's hidden in my cottage if you would like to see it."

"No, that won't be necessary." In all their years of friendship, they'd never kept secrets from each other. Of course, with him being in jail and a war raging, communication had been next to impossible.

But even if Madeleine had been married to JP, that didn't explain why she'd accused him of killing his best friend.

"What makes you think I had something to do with JP's death?"

Her head snapped up, her eyes flashing a challenge. "Because if it hadn't been for the telegram you sent him, he would never have walked into that trap. You set him up!"

"What telegram?"

"He told me a diamond he'd purchased, *le Coeur Bleu*, was too risky to keep in France after the Germans invaded. He received a telegram from you telling him you had arranged a meeting with a very important diamond buyer who would take the diamond off his hands and smuggle it out of the country. He went to the meeting place, and the Gestapo was waiting for him." Madeleine blinked, holding back tears. "They arrested him. Jean Philippe's friends in the police force found out he'd been arrested and got me out of Paris immediately. Not long after, I received word that the Nazis had executed Jean Philippe. They accused him of helping a Jewish family to escape to England. I didn't know

31

anything about what he'd done for that family, but I was very proud of him."

"I was proud of him, too," Hunter said quietly. He told them about the cryptic telegram he'd received from Jean Philippe in the spring of 1940. Guilt still haunted him. Instead of wiring the money, he should have tried to persuade JP not to get involved.

If he was truly honest with himself, the temptation of owning such a magnificent diamond at the bargain basement price the refugee requested for it, had proved too much for him to resist.

"The Heartstone, is that not the nickname given to *le Coeur Bleu*?" Monsieur Gagnon asked.

"Yes, that's right." Hunter had spent the years before the war working as a diamond broker, buying and selling diamonds across Europe and in London and New York. Jean Philippe had known of his expertise and of his contacts in the diamond world.

"What did Jean Philippe mean by "times two"?

Hunter shook his head. "I had no idea. I still don't. But I trusted JP completely, so I wired him the money to purchase the diamond. I never heard from him again."

"He may not have contacted you, but you contacted him!" Madeleine stepped closer. "I saw the telegram myself. I saw your name on it."

"When did JP receive this telegram?" Hunter asked.

Madeleine closed her eyes and swallowed. "I will never forget the day. It was August 15, 1940."

"Madeleine, by August 1940 I was a guest in His Majesty's prison at Pentonville. I couldn't have sent that telegram."

"That's true," Monsieur Gagnon said. "The intelligence I received on Monsieur Smith from the SOE said he was arrested for jewel theft in July 1940 and remained in custody until Monsieur Campbell had him released."

Madeleine turned cold blue eyes on him. "So, you are

merely a thief, then. That gives me very little comfort, monsieur. My husband was twice the man you are."

"Yes, he was."

Jean Philippe had always been the better man. Hunter had known that from the time they were ten-year-olds living together in the ambassador's residence in Paris. JP had pulled him back from the brink of trouble more times than he could remember. He was Hunter's conscience, his touchstone.

"The only reason I came to France was because of Jean Philippe. He had unfinished business with *le Coeur Bleu*. I intend to finish it for him."

Madeleine lifted her chin. "Yes. So do I."

Chapter Five

Hunter followed Madeleine into her cottage. She lit an oil lamp, illuminating a small, sparsely furnished room containing a table and three chairs, a woodburning cookstove, and a tiny bed. Then she set about lighting the stove.

"I don't have much food here, just some bread and cheese. I'll put on some tea."

Hunter's interest was immediately piqued. "You have tea? I thought it was pretty hard to come by these days."

"I'm sorry. Black tea *is* very hard to come by. This is an herbal tea made of dried rose hips. Madame Gagnon prepared it."

"Oh, I see." He tried to hide his disappointment. Of all the things that were in short supply, he most missed tea. He'd kill for a really good cup of steaming hot, black English tea.

She sensed his disappointment. "Sorry about that. I haven't had real tea in months."

"Don't worry about it. Madame Gagnon's tea will be fine. Can I help with anything?"

She handed him a baguette without looking at him. "You can slice this. There's a knife in the drawer by the stove."

In a short time the tea was steeped and their simple supper laid out on the table. They ate in silence, the tension thick between them. *Unless we find a way to get past the awkwardness, our mission is doomed. Perhaps if we concentrate on the work at hand.* Hunter finished his tea and set his mug on the table.

34

"Tell me about the chateau. Where is General Dietrich keeping the diamond?"

"We believe it's in a safe in his private office. I'll show you."

She went to the bureau, pulled some paper and a pencil from a drawer, and, returning to the table, began to draw a rough map.

"The office is on the main floor of the chateau, in the west wing. The general uses this room as his private retreat."

Madeleine drew doors, windows and hallways on her map, along with the location of the guard posts in that wing of the chateau. "There is always a guard stationed in front of the general's office door. We don't know for certain that the diamond is there, but the fact that the general feels the need to guard the room seems to indicate something of value inside."

"Have you been inside this room?"

"*Oui,* many times." She grabbed another piece of paper and began to draw the interior of the office. "There's an enormous desk in the middle of the room, facing the door. Three walls have floor-to-ceiling bookcases, and two large windows take up the fourth wall." Hunter picked up the drawing and examined it closely. Something was missing.

"Where's the safe?"

Madeleine frowned. "I'm not exactly sure. Collette said she saw a wall safe behind one of the bookshelves, but I've never seen it myself."

"I thought you said you've been in the office many times."

Her eyes flashed. "I have, to clean and dust. But I've never been left to explore on my own. Either the general or one of his guards is always there."

Agitated, Hunter jumped to his feet and began pacing. "That's great. I'm supposed to break into a room that's constantly guarded to retrieve a diamond that may or may not be located in a safe that perhaps might be hidden behind one of several bookcases, if it exists at all."

Madeleine rose to her full height, her mouth set in a thin, angry line. "If you would just listen for a moment, I will tell you how we will get into the office and find the safe."

Her blue eyes threw icy darts at him, her chin set at a defiant angle as she stared him down, chest heaving. Her anger was breathtaking.

Hunter swallowed and averted his gaze, resuming his seat.

"*Pardon,* Madeleine. I'm sorry. What do you have planned?"

Madeleine stood for a few seconds longer, her knuckles white as she clutched the edge of the table. At last she drew a deep breath and sat, closing her eyes for a few moments before speaking.

"My position as a housemaid allows me to observe much in the chateau. The soldier who has been on guard duty in front of the office door for the last few weeks makes a habit of visiting the water closet down the hall for an extended period every day right after lunch. The office is unguarded for at least ten minutes. I propose we break into the office tomorrow while the guard is away and have a look around."

Her plan made sense. A reconnaissance mission would allow him to familiarize himself with the room and to find the elusive safe. When the time came to steal the diamond, he'd know the make and model of the safe and the best way to break into the room.

"It's a good idea. You're sure this guard will be away from his post for at least ten minutes?"

"Yes, very sure. I thank God every day for his regular bathroom habits."

Hunter laughed at her unexpected show of humor. Madeleine smiled as well, and for a moment the tension between them dissipated. Then her smile faded.

"Another good reason to check out the office tomorrow is because General Dietrich and his aide are scheduled to be in Paris for a meeting until late in the afternoon. We won't have to worry about him for a while."

From the cloud that passed over her face Hunter knew there wasn't a moment Madeleine didn't worry about the general. An overpowering urge assailed him. He wanted to pull her into his arms and whisper reassurances, tell her everything would be all right, that he would look after her. *What is it about this woman that makes me want to protect her?*

He pushed away the fanciful thoughts. He was here to do a job, nothing more. The only thing he and Madeleine had in common was Jean Philippe. He'd be well advised to remember that.

"Look, Madeleine, this is difficult for both of us. But at least now we both know where we stand. We're both here because of Jean Philippe. Let's just try to do this job so that he can rest in peace."

Madeleine nodded. "Yes, you're right." She looked somewhere over his shoulder, not meeting his eyes.

"I know you find it uncomfortable to have me in your home, and I'm sorry about that. When I saw General Dietrich with you, there didn't seem to be any other way but to tell him we were married." Just thinking about the general touching Madeleine made him want to put his fist through a wall. If he'd had his gun with him, he would have shot the bastard.

And then they'd both be dead.

Her lips curled in a brief smile. "I'm glad you did. I'd told him before that I was married, but he didn't care. He didn't even care when my husband magically appeared. The only thing that put him off was the thought that I was pregnant. How did you know that would keep him away from me?"

"I didn't. I simply hoped the thought of a pregnant

mistress who vomited every morning would prove too distressing to his delicate constitution."

"I'm glad it worked." She looked into his eyes. "Thank you."

"You're welcome."

She clasped her hands in front of her on the table, her brow creasing as she stared at them. "Sometimes I can still feel Jean Philippe. I can feel his warmth, his love, all around me, embracing me like a warm blanket. I feel him in my heart."

Hunter reached across the table and covered her hands with his. "I feel him, too. He's always there telling me the right thing to do."

She looked up, and a crystal tear slid down her cheek. "I loved him."

"So did I."

****

Madeleine still didn't like the idea of sharing her small cottage with Hunter. Since the cottage was essentially one room, the feeling was far too intimate, as if they were sharing a bedroom. Though she'd prepared a pallet for him on the floor on the other side of the room, Hunter filled the cottage with his presence. No matter how quiet or unobtrusive he tried to be, she couldn't ignore him or forget he was there.

She'd spent almost two years hating him. But the evidence suggested she'd been wrong about him all this time. And if she were honest with herself, now that she'd met Hunter she couldn't imagine him harming Jean Philippe in any way.

In fact, this evening, when he wasn't infuriating her, she'd found herself liking him. Very strange.

There was still one question to be answered. Who had sent the telegram from England that had led Jean Philippe to his death? Madeleine would not rest until she knew.

She threw a sheet over the clothesline, dividing the

cottage in two and giving her a modicum of privacy. Still, she felt apprehensive as she lit the oil lamp next to her bed and poured warm water into a basin, preparing her toilette for the evening.

"Is there anything I can get for you before I go to bed? Water, perhaps?" she asked from behind the protection of the sheet.

"No, I'm fine. Thank you."

Madeleine heard the rustling of blankets as he settled on his palette. "I'm sorry I don't have something more comfortable for you."

"Don't worry about it. I've slept on far worse."

She sighed, her nerves on edge. After washing her face and hands, she slipped off her skirt and unbuttoned her blouse. Just as she unhooked her brassiere, she heard a groan from the other side of the room.

"Hunter? Are you all right?"

"Yes, I'm fine. Go to sleep." His voice sounded strained.

Madeleine quickly donned her nightgown, the worn flannel covering her completely from neck to ankle, before extinguishing the oil lamp.

"Goodnight, Hunter."

"Goodnight, Madeleine."

She lay awake listening to his breathing. It had been a long time since she'd shared a room, or a bed, and it was disconcerting. But it was also comforting, in a strange way. Somehow she felt safe with Hunter in her cottage.

After a while his breathing changed and she knew he slept. Madeleine snuggled deeper into her blankets and fell immediately into a dreamless sleep.

****

The next day at lunch, Madeleine took her usual place at the kitchen table with the other staff. She tried to eat, but her food tasted like sawdust. The thought of breaking into the general's office after lunch terrified her. Her stomach clenched, threatening to dislodge anything she choked down. If they were caught...

Hunter entered the kitchen with the rest of the gardeners, grinning when he saw her. She felt an answering smile tug at her lips. Madeleine watched as he filled a bowl with soup from the pot on the stove. He brought it with him to the table and came to stand behind Madeleine.

"Mademoiselle," he said, addressing the housemaid sitting beside her. "Perhaps you would be so good as to exchange seats with me. It's been a long time since I've had a chance to eat lunch with my wife."

The housemaid gave Madeleine a wink before smiling up at Hunter. "*Oui,* of course, Monsieur Lemay. Anything for love."

The others chuckled as the housemaid took her bowl and moved to the other side of the table while Hunter sat beside Madeleine. He leaned in close and whispered in her ear.

"You must eat, Madame Lemay. You need to keep up your strength."

A shiver rippled down Madeleine's spine as she stared into his dark, laughing eyes, unable to look away.

"*Oui*, Monsieur Lemay."

He kissed her, barely a brushing of his lips over hers, but enough to cause a jolt of electricity to course through her body. Her fingertips tingled, desperately wanting to feel the stubble of his beard, the silkiness of his thick, wavy hair. The others at the table hooted in laughter.

"Monsieur Lemay! You have to wait until tonight for that!"

"Madeleine, you've got a charmer there!"

Madeleine's face heated in embarrassment. Hunter simply winked at her and, grinning, proceeded to devour his lunch. Madeleine dipped her spoon into her own soup and found she now had an appetite for it.

He finished eating and, with a squeeze to her shoulder,

left the table at twenty minutes to one. At fifteen minutes before one Madeleine excused herself, as well. With shaking hands, she assembled her supplies of beeswax and soft cloths, her excuse should anyone question her reason for being near the general's private office. She made her way toward the agreed-upon meeting place down the hall from the office. Hunter was waiting for her.

"Did you have any trouble getting away?" he asked.

"No, but let's make this quick before anyone misses us."

They watched from a safe distance as the guard hurried from his post at the office door to the water closet down the hall. As soon as he rounded a corner, Madeleine and Hunter left their hiding place and slipped quietly inside the room, using the housekeeping key Madeleine had taken.

Madeleine stood guard at the door, watching for any of the general's staff. In a glance at Hunter she saw he was meticulously feeling around the bookcases, looking for the one that would open to reveal the safe.

"Hurry!" she whispered. "The guard will be back any minute."

"I'm well aware, Madeleine," he replied. "There must be a release here somewhere. Ah. There we go."

With another quick glance back into the room Madeleine could see one of the bookcase panels opening to reveal a small safe imbedded in the wall. Hunter examined it. The sight of his long, lean fingers stroking the door, the handle, the keyhole, mesmerized her. The memory of his touch assaulted her without warning. She knew his hands possessed strength yet could be remarkably gentle. How would those clever hands respond in the throes of passion?

Brisk footsteps echoed outside on the marble hallway. The guard was on his way back to his post. Madeleine's heart lodged in her throat.

"The guard's coming! Hurry!"

Hunter quickly closed the bookcase, making sure it

clicked back into place. He came to her side.

"If we make a run for it, he'll see us and know for certain we've been searching the room. Leave the door open a crack."

"Are you crazy?" Fear turned her knees to water.

"Probably." Hunter looked deeply into her eyes. "Forgive me, Madeleine."

Her breath caught at his intense expression. "For what?"

"This."

His mouth descended on hers with insistent passion, taking her by surprise. The beeswax fell to the floor with a small clatter. He pulled her tightly against him, his arms holding her securely. He turned her, pushing her up against a wall, his mouth raining hot, wet kisses down her neck. Her hands clutched at him, pulling him closer. For a moment she forgot the danger, the mission, her own name. There was only Hunter and the feel of him in her arms, on her lips.

The door opened with a bang as it crashed against the wall. "*Was macht?* What is this?" the guard shouted in German. "What are you doing in here?"

He pointed his semi-automatic rifle at them. Madeleine's heart raced in fear. She instinctively turned her face into Hunter's chest. He wrapped a protective arm around her.

"My wife," he said in French. "We've been apart too long."

Madeleine knew this guard spoke no French. Did Hunter have any German? Even if he did, he was wise not to make it known to the guard. Better to be thought of as a simple French gardener.

The guard looked them up and down, taking in Madeleine's disheveled hair and clothes. A slow smile spread over face.

"You French. You think of nothing but sex. *Schnell*. Go quickly." The guard motioned with his rifle.

Madeleine hastily picked up her can of beeswax and her

cloth from the floor and followed Hunter out of the room. They were both aware of the guard watching them as they headed down the hall.

Hunter stopped at a door that led into the garden and turned to her, taking her hand. Three vertical lines of worry marred his smooth brow.

"Are you all right?"

"I'll be fine. Is he still watching?"

"Yes. Can you smile at me, make him think you're madly in love?"

She managed to dredge up a sunny smile. He placed one finger under her chin, tilting her face to look in her eyes.

"Good girl. About back there, I'm sorry. Did I hurt you?"

"No, of course not."

He closed his eyes briefly. When he reopened them she caught a flash of anguish. "Good. Jean Philippe was my best friend. I don't know—"

"Shhh." She placed her finger on his mouth. She couldn't talk about this right now, couldn't hear his feelings. She'd shocked herself with her response to him. Was it just her body's reaction to the feel of a handsome man in her arms, or was it something more?

She pushed the questions away, unwilling to think about them.

"I'll meet you after work in front of the chateau, and we'll walk home together," she said. "He'll expect me to kiss you goodbye."

"Yes."

Madeleine leaned close and touched her lips to his. His lips were soft and warm, and she sighed as she stepped even closer. His big hands clutched her shoulders but held her with infinite tenderness. She felt safe in Hunter's arms. Safe and warm and cherished.

He broke away first, the look on his face unreadable. She saw him swallow, his gaze not quite meeting hers. "I'll see you later."

"Goodbye." He slipped out the door and disappeared, leaving Madeleine feeling alone and bereft for a moment.

She quickly shook off the feeling. There was no time for such emotions.

Madeleine glanced at the guard, who still watched from in front of the office door. He lifted his rifle in salute. She glanced away and hurried off. *He won't tell anyone we've been inside the office because then he'll have to explain why he was away from his post.* She could dismiss the guard from her mind.

She wished she could dismiss Hunter as easily. But he had opened the door to emotions and responses that had lain dormant for almost two years, ever since Jean Philippe's death.

Now it was open, she had no idea how to close this door again.

Chapter Six

For the rest of the afternoon, Madeleine busied herself dusting and mopping the bedrooms on the third floor, keeping a careful eye out for General Dietrich. Thoughts of the kiss she'd shared with Hunter continued to swirl in her head. The softness of his lips against hers and the passion of his touch played themselves over and over in her memory. Even his scent seemed to float on the breeze wafting in through the open window of the guest bedroom. She closed her eyes and moaned. Was there no escaping the man?

Madeleine punched a pillow into submission, telling herself she had responded so ardently to his kisses only because she'd been alone for so long. She would have responded the same way to any man's kiss. It had nothing to do with him.

The door opened and Madeleine stiffened in fear, terrified the general had found her again. She nearly wept with relief when Madame Beauchamp, head housekeeper, entered the room.

"Are you nearly finished here, Madeleine? I need you downstairs to help polish the silverware."

"*Oui,* madame. I just need to finish mopping the floor."

"Good. As soon as you finish, come downstairs to the kitchen and find me. I'll show you what to do."

"*Oui,* madame."

Madame Beauchamp was about to leave when they heard the general's voice in the hallway. The older woman quietly closed the bedroom door and turned to Madeleine.

"He must have arrived home early from his meeting in Paris. He's got his eye on you. It's not safe for you to be here on your own," she whispered. "Quickly! Come with me."

She led Madeleine toward a wall of bookcases. Shoving aside some books, she depressed a lever that caused one column of bookshelves to open, revealing a door to a dark tunnel. Madame Beauchamp reached into her pocket and pulled out a small flashlight that she pressed into Madeleine's hands. She then pushed her through the opening behind the bookshelf.

"The tunnel will take you to an alcove just outside the main ballroom. From there you can take the back stairs to the kitchen. Go! Hurry!"

The bookshelf door closed in her face. For a few seconds Madeleine stood completely still in the pitch dark, her heart hammering. Then survival mode kicked in, and she knew she needed to get moving.

She switched on the flashlight and discovered that she stood at the top of a set of steep, winding wooden stairs. Carefully, she made her way down the stairs to a landing and walked for some time along a narrow passageway constructed between the walls of the chateau. Madeleine wondered if the passageway had been used originally as a means of escaping from enemies or if its purpose was simply a bit of whimsy, a way of playing an elaborate game of hide and seek.

Whatever the purpose, she wished they'd made the passage a little wider.

"The walls are *not* closing in on me," she whispered, desperately trying to convince herself. The narrower the passage became, the harder it was to breathe. "I will *not* be stuck in here forever."

Finally she saw a doorway up ahead. She prayed it led to the alcove Madame Beauchamp spoke of because, however grateful she felt for her escape from General Dietrich, she would be even more grateful to escape the cramped passageway.

The doorway was small, perhaps two feet square, and located near the floor. Madeleine got down on her knees and examined the tiny door, looking for the mechanism to open it. Her searching fingers found a button. The door made a popping sound as it opened outward. Just as Madame Beauchamp had said, she was in the alcove of the ballroom. She peered out from a crack between the door and its frame, listening. All was quiet. The general used the ballroom as the main office for his staff, as well as a place to hold meetings and entertain guests, but today it sounded deserted. She breathed a sigh of relief. Opening the door as wide as it would go, she crawled through on her belly.

Once into the alcove, Madeleine pushed the door shut. The door fit inside a piece of paneling in the wall and was totally indistinguishable from any other panel. She dusted herself off and made her way toward the back stairs to the kitchen.

"*Fraulein*, what are you doing here?"

Madeleine whirled to see Lieutenant Hauser, one of the general's aides.

"I...I came to see if you needed me to dust in the ballroom."

Hauser narrowed his eyes. "That won't be necessary. Someone cleaned the ballroom yesterday. Didn't they tell you?"

"Oh, I'm sorry, monsieur. I must have confused the days. I'm sorry to have disturbed you."

She inclined her head and made an about-turn, her heart racing with the fear that he would stop her and demand to know what she was *really* doing just outside the ballroom. But he let her go without a word. Madeleine sprinted down the back stairs into the relative safety of the kitchen. She was relieved to find the cook and her assistant there. A moment later Madame Beauchamp arrived, looking completely calm, as if she threw housemaids into secret passageways every day of the week.

"Ah, there you are, Madeleine," she said with a smile. "You're just in time to help me polish the silver."

"*Oui*, madame."

Madeleine sat at the table in front of the silver utensils that had been laid out there. Madame Beauchamp sat beside her and handed her the silver polish.

"*Merci*, madame."

Madeleine tried to convey her gratitude in her eyes. If the general had found her alone again, even her pretend pregnancy might not have deterred him.

Madame Beauchamp smiled. "You're very welcome."

****

Neither Madeleine nor Hunter said anything as they walked back to her cottage after work. When she waved to some of the neighbors as they passed, Hunter realized that Madame Gagnon's advice to live together in Madeleine's house had been sound. People were watching them, and though they planned to be together here for only a few days, those days were critical. Everyone from General Dietrich and the staff at the chateau to the little old lady next door had to believe they were married. Their fake marriage had to look real.

Hunter just wished it didn't feel so real.

After Natasha's betrayal, he'd sworn he'd never trust another woman again. But Madeleine made him forget all those promises he'd made to himself. Perhaps if she'd been anyone else, and they lived in another time and place, something good and strong and lasting could have happened between them.

But Madeleine wasn't anyone else. She was the widow of his best friend, a man he'd loved from childhood with all his heart. A man he would have given his life to protect. How could he dishonor Jean Philippe's memory by lusting after his wife?

"You're very quiet," she said.

"Sorry. I've been thinking about the mission," he lied.

"Yes, so have I. Do you think you will have any trouble with the safe?"

"I don't know. It's new and German, a model I haven't worked with before."

"You mean you've never cracked this kind of safe before?"

"No, I haven't."

"But you've opened lots of others, right? You have lots of experience cracking safes?"

"Yes, I have."

He knew his skills were essential to this mission, but admitting to Madeleine that he'd been a thief in his past made him feel less a man.

How could she ever feel anything for him when she'd been married to a man like Jean Philippe, a man who upheld the law, an honest man?

"That's good. Hopefully you'll be able to figure out this one, too," Madeleine said with a nod. "The quicker you can crack the safe and get the diamond, the faster you'll be done. Where do you want me to be while you're opening the safe?"

He looked at her in shock. "I don't want you anywhere near that safe."

She lifted her chin in defiance. "Don't be ridiculous. At the very least you need me to keep watch at the door."

"There won't be anything to watch. We know a German guard will be posted outside the door. All I need is for you to slip into the office sometime during the day when the guard isn't around and make sure the window is unlocked."

"Yes, but—"

"No buts, Maddie. I don't want you there. I have enough to worry about."

"What did you call me?"

He stared at her in confusion until he realized he'd shortened her name. "Oh. I called you Maddie. Sorry. It's sort of an American custom to shorten a person's name."

"Like the way you used to call Jean Philippe 'JP'?"

He looked away, feeling like he'd just taken a knife to the heart. "Yeah. Like that."

"He loved you, you know. He talked about you all the time, especially about the things you did as kids."

Hunter couldn't answer her. How could he, when his throat was clogged with guilt and shame for wanting JP's wife? And knowing that someone had used him to get to JP?

"I understand now you couldn't have sent that telegram," Madeleine said. She squeezed his hand, making Hunter turn to look into her eyes. "Someone used your name to trick Jean Philippe. They used the fact that he trusted you. It's not your fault."

Hunter looked away. He wished he could make himself believe that. Someone had used the knowledge that he and JP were best friends. Someone who also knew, somehow, that JP was in possession of *le Coeur Bleu*. Hunter had his suspicions as to the identity of this someone, but no concrete evidence. And even if he could prove what he suspected, what good would it do now? It wouldn't bring JP back.

They arrived at Madeleine's door, and Hunter held it open for her. She peeled off her jacket and slung it over one of the chairs. When she removed the ribbon fastening her ponytail, her long dark tresses cascaded down her back in shiny waves. Hunter's mouth went instantly dry.

"Oh, how nice! Madame Gagnon has left us some supper." She opened a bottle of wine. "Would you like some?"

"Sure."

She poured wine into two glasses and set them on the table. "There's a baguette, some cheese, and cold sliced beef. Are you hungry?"

More than you know. "Famished."

Madeleine brought some plates and utensils to the table, and in a few moments they were eating. When she finished, she pushed her plate away and got up from the table.

"I want to show you something."

She went to a trunk and pulled out a small wooden box. Setting it on the table, she removed another smaller box, wrapped in a colorful silk scarf, from inside the wooden box and handed it to him.

"Do you remember this?"

Hunter peeled back the layers of silk to reveal a Japanese puzzle box, about the size and shape of a small brick. With a smile, he replied, "Of course. JP's mother's puzzle box. It was her prized possession."

The box was made of many tiny pieces of wood of different colors and species, fitted together to form an intricate mosaic pattern. The wooden pieces together formed a box that was then beautifully lacquered. The puzzle of the box was that it had a hidden compartment that could be opened only if one knew the right combination of moves. Since the box was made up of many pieces, sliding some of the parts on one end allowed the other end to be moved slightly. This partially unlocked a side panel, which allowed other pieces to be moved. These in turn partially unlocked the top. This pattern continued, moving around the box, until the top panel finally slid open, revealing the secret compartment.

"Jean Philippe gave it to me on our wedding day, along with the necklace."

"And your wedding band, of course," he said.

Madeleine twisted the ring. "Actually, this is my mother's ring. Jean Philippe and I didn't have enough money for rings when we married. We were saving to buy them."

Profound sadness clouded her expression. Hunter's gut twisted at her distress. *Stupid fool! Has she not suffered enough? Must you remind her at every turn how much she's lost?*

"Hélène never let me touch the box. Do you know how to open it?"

She smiled, visibly shaking off her dark memories.

"Yes, I do. Jean Philippe showed me how, but I haven't opened it since he...since he died."

Hunter noticed the hitch in her voice, felt it deep in his heart. *If only I could say something to ease her pain.* But he knew that only time could do that.

Time and perhaps revenge.

He rewrapped the puzzle box and handed it back to her. She carefully placed it in the wooden box once more and then brought out a much smaller box from her knapsack.

"I think you'll recognize this, too. Open it."

He did as she asked. Inside the box, wrapped in folds of soft, white cloth, lay Jean Philippe's pocket watch, the one handed down to him from his father. As he cradled the watch in his hand, a kaleidoscope of memories bombarded him: eating fresh croissants in Hélène Bertrand's kitchen, fighting off bullies at school, playing kickball in the courtyard of the ambassador's residence...

He could almost hear JP's voice:

She belongs to me.

Hunter rewrapped the watch and placed it carefully back in the box. He wished he could pack away his memories as neatly.

"Jean Philippe once told me you'd rescued his father's watch when it was stolen from him, but he never told me how you did it."

Hunter couldn't help but smile again. "Ah, yes. The beginning of my life of crime."

"How old were you?"

"We were twelve. Both of us were attending Madame La Roche's Private School. To get in, you had to be either an embassy brat or come from old French money."

"You were the embassy brat, but how did Jean Philippe get in? He and his mother had no money."

"True, but he had smarts and he had connections, namely my father. He paid for JP's tuition." He sighed, his finger touching the rim of his wine glass. "I always wondered if my father paid the tuition because he was having an affair with Hélène."

"Did that bother you?"

"That they were having an affair? No, not at all. I had a twelve-year-old's fantasy about my father marrying Hélène and her being my mom and JP being my brother. But it was just a fantasy."

He shook off the memory of his lonely childhood. "But you wanted to know about the watch."

Madeleine smiled that beautiful smile that lit up her face. *Sunshine*. She reminded him of sunshine.

"Yes, I'd like to hear the story of the watch."

"All right. JP and I were at Madame La Roche's school with the cream of Paris society. Unfortunately, some of that cream was a little spoiled."

Madeleine laughed, and for a moment he enjoyed the happy sound of it.

"Go on, go on. Tell me the rest."

"There was a group of boys who were the worst. They didn't give me too much trouble, because I was the American ambassador's son, but they found out that JP's mother was merely a housekeeper, and they taunted him mercilessly. Pierre Revier, he was the worst. His father was some high-and-mighty banker, and nothing mattered more to Pierre than how much money a person had. Unless of course it was who your father was, and how powerful your family was.

"One day when we were outside for gym class, Pierre broke into JP's locker and stole this watch. JP carried it with him everywhere in those days. He probably told you his father died in the Great War?"

When Madeleine nodded, he continued. "It was the only thing he had of his father's, and it meant the world to him."

"How did you know Pierre was the one who stole it?"

"Because he told JP. Flaunted it, actually. Said there was nothing JP could do about it because the headmistress wouldn't believe him, and even if she did she wouldn't punish Pierre because of who his father was."

"The little brat!" Madeleine exclaimed.

Hunter chuckled. "Precisely. Pierre even told JP where he was hiding the watch—in the safe in his father's study at his house."

"That was cheeky."

"It was. In Pierre's mind, there was no way JP could get the watch from his father's safe, so he was free to taunt JP all he wanted. I, on the other hand, had a different plan."

"I can just imagine," Madeleine said with a grin.

"I spent a lot of my time in the kitchen at the ambassador's residence, so I knew all the staff. One of the gardeners was an ex-con and had served time for theft. The man was an expert safe-cracker. Gaston, this gardener, could pick any lock, open any safe. I first found this out when I lost the key for my bike lock and he used a pick to open it in about ten seconds flat. When Pierre stole JP's watch, I blackmailed Gaston into teaching me how to open a safe. I told him if he didn't teach me everything he knew, I'd tell my father he was an ex-con."

"That's terrible, Hunter!"

"I know, but I had no intention of telling my father anything. Gaston's secret was safe with me. He just didn't know it."

"So Gaston taught you to crack safes?"

"He did, and he was a very good teacher. We must have opened my father's safe thirty times before he was satisfied. When I knew I could open my father's safe with my eyes closed, I made my plans for Pierre."

"What a devious little boy you were!"

"I had no intention of letting Pierre get away with stealing JP's only memento of his father."

Madeleine gave him a strange look. "You were very determined to help him, weren't you?"

"Yes. Nobody treats the people I love badly and gets

away with it."

She smiled. "So then you broke into Pierre's father's safe and stole back the watch?"

"Not quite."

"Not quite? What do you mean?"

"My parents were invited to a fancy party at a rich woman's house. I can't remember her name. My parents never took me to such things. Probably afraid I'd do something to embarrass them, and they were probably right. Anyway, Pierre starting bragging at school how his parents were taking him to this fancy party. He went on about it for days. And that's when I got my bright idea."

"Your bright idea?"

"To pay Pierre back for all the mean things he'd done. The rich lady's house was around the corner from the ambassador's residence, so as soon as my parents left and Hélène thought I was safely in bed, I climbed out the window and rode my bike to the rich lady's house. The staff at my house had been talking about all the fancy jewels this lady had, so I figured if I took one of her necklaces and put it in Pierre's safe he'd get the blame for it."

"*Mon Dieu*, Hunter, you didn't!"

"I'm afraid I did. I climbed through a window into the lady's bedroom. She'd been so kind as to leave some of her jewelry lying around on her dressing table. I grabbed a necklace and left. Then I biked to Pierre's house, climbed through a window there, and opened his father's safe. It was a little different from my father's safe, but it didn't take me long to pick the lock. I put the necklace inside but left JP's watch. I was afraid if I took it everyone would think JP had broken into the safe. I climbed out the window again, biked home and crawled into my bed. No one ever knew I'd left."

"Did Jean Philippe know about any of this?"

"No, not till years later. I knew if I told him he'd try to talk me out of it. Worse, he'd tell Hélène. I thought up this little scheme all by myself."

Madeleine touched the box containing the watch. "Obviously Jean Philippe got his watch back. How did that happen?"

"The next day it was all over the papers that the rich lady's necklace had been stolen. Turns out the necklace I'd lifted was worth a fortune. The police were completely stumped. They were questioning all the staff at her house, figuring that one of them had to be guilty. I didn't like them harassing the staff and I wanted to point the finger at Pierre, so I sent the police an anonymous note, written on my father's secretary's typewriter, telling them that Pierre had been seen entering the rich lady's bedroom."

"*Sacre bleu!*" Madeleine put her hand to her forehead. "How old were you, again?"

"Twelve."

"When I was twelve, I was playing with dolls. What happened next?"

"The police actually took my note seriously. They questioned Pierre and his father and mother. His father was furious and threatened to sue the entire Paris police force. Apparently the Chief of Police didn't like being threatened, so he asked a judge for a search warrant to search Pierre's house. When they opened the safe they found the necklace and JP's watch. They traced the watch to JP because of the inscription engraved on the back, and returned it to him. JP, of course, told the police the story about how Pierre had taken his watch. He was delighted to get it back, and I was happy for him."

Madeleine tilted her head, regarding him carefully. "You don't sound very happy."

"I'm not happy, Madeleine. Pierre was expelled from school and his family shamed. They lost practically their whole fortune defending themselves in court. But the worst thing was that Pierre's father believed he really had stolen the necklace. His father was ashamed of him for the rest of his life. And it was all because of me."

Madeleine covered his hand with hers. "You were twelve, Hunter. You didn't understand what would happen."

Her eyes were very kind, giving him the absolution he'd never been able to give himself. "Perhaps. But at least I learned my lesson. I never stole anything again."

Her eyebrows rose in disbelief. "Really? You were in jail for theft. They caught you red-handed."

Suddenly it became very important that she saw him as something other than a thief. "I was putting the jewels back."

"Putting them back? What do you mean?"

"I was in love. With a beautiful Russian émigrée named Natasha. We were at a party one night in London when she suddenly started to cry. She said that a lady across the room was wearing jewelry that had belonged to her grandmother. The Bolsheviks had stolen it during the revolution. Her grandmother had been too old to flee with the rest of the family when they left Moscow, and she'd been killed. Natasha was inconsolable. I took her home and I promised I'd get the jewels back for her."

"By stealing them?"

Hunter averted his eyes, ashamed. "There didn't seem to be any other way. In my civilian life I was a trader in diamonds and other precious and semi-precious stones. I knew the value of this suite of diamonds—a necklace, earrings and a hair ornament—and I knew there was no way I could afford to buy them for her. They had been rumored to have come out of Russia after the revolution, so I had no reason to doubt Natasha."

In hindsight, he should have seen all the warning signs: Natasha's insistence that they go to the party that night, her close relationship with her "brother," her smooth explanations to any of his questions. But he'd been too in love and too blind to see past her façade.

"I began planning the heist, but I was pretty rusty. I hadn't cracked a safe in a long time, except to amuse friends at parties. But that was just for fun. I occasionally used the lock picks Gaston gave me to open a door when I locked myself out of my flat." He didn't add that he'd become a master at picking locks at the Swiss boarding school where his parents had sent him during his high school years. The place was like a prison, and he'd used his picks to come and go at will. It had been the loneliest time of his life. "Other than that, I was clean. I had no interest in causing disruption to people's lives again."

"So because you were out of practice, you were caught as you were trying to steal the jewels."

"No. As I said, I was caught when I tried to return them." Hunter leaned back in his seat and let out a breath. Remembering the humiliation and the pain of betrayal he'd felt at that time was difficult enough, but telling Madeleine about it made it doubly so. "I planned the robbery down to the last detail and prepared to break into the woman's flat on an evening she was to be out for dinner with friends. Then I received word from my sources that the woman's plans had changed and she was planning her dinner engagement with her friends on the Friday evening instead of Saturday. I had to move faster than I'd expected, and there was no time to inform Natasha.

"On the Friday evening, I broke into the woman's apartment, opened her safe, and slipped out again without being seen. I raced to Natasha's apartment to surprise her, anxious to see her reaction when I presented her with the suite of diamonds. I knew she'd be thrilled to have them restored to her family once more." Hunter also expected to be rewarded with the glorious sexual escapades Natasha had tantalized him with but up to that point had withheld.

"When I got to her apartment I found her in bed with her so-called brother."

"Her brother?" Madeleine stared at him in disbelief.

Hunter grimaced, remembering his own shock and disgust. "It turned out the fellow was Natasha's husband. I found out later they'd been stealing jewels all across Europe but the police hadn't managed to catch up with them."

"What did you do?"

"I told Natasha exactly what I thought of her. She wanted me to give her the jewels, but I refused. She'd tricked me, and I told her I was going to put the jewels back where I found them. With any luck I could have them back in place before they were missed. I also told her I'd make sure everyone in our social circle knew she was nothing but a fake and a thief. That was a mistake. She made a call to the police, pretending to be the woman whose jewels I'd stolen. She told them someone was in her apartment trying to break into her safe. The cops were there in minutes and, as you said, they caught me red-handed."

"I gather they didn't believe you were trying to put the jewels back."

"No. Natasha and her husband skipped the country before the police could question them, leaving me to take the rap." Hunter took a deep breath and let it out slowly. "So that's it. You've now heard the story of my life."

"And an interesting story it is." She absently fingered Hélène's necklace at her throat. "Monsieur Gagnon told me *le Coeur Bleu* is said to be cursed."

"They say it has magical powers, as well."

"Magical powers? What is the diamond purported to do? Monsieur Gagnon was not specific."

"It's all just superstition, a crazy story made up to explain things people couldn't understand."

"Tell me." When he hesitated, she touched his hand. "I need to know what Jean Philippe died for."

Hunter nodded. "The diamond was mined in India in the 1700s. A European is reputed to have stolen it from the miners who found it. Soon after, he was trampled to death by a rogue elephant. That's when rumors of the curse began. Since then, owners who bought or inherited the diamond fair and square enjoyed much happiness and long life. However, anyone who stole, used trickery, or killed to obtain the diamond either died a horrible, painful death, or was somehow tricked himself."

"That doesn't explain Jean Philippe's death," she said. "He bought the diamond fair and square. He used no trickery. Why did he die?"

Hunter had no answers for her. "It's just a superstition, Madeleine. It doesn't mean anything."

"Perhaps the man who had him killed will suffer such a fate himself." Hatred twisted her beautiful face. "I wish a horrible, painful death on General Dietrich."

"Dietrich? Dietrich had Jean Philippe killed?" Hunter's heart began to pound.

"Yes. I thought you knew. He was stationed in Paris at the time, with the Gestapo. Somehow he found out that Jean Philippe had the diamond. He received a big promotion after arresting him for smuggling Jews out of France. He just neglected to tell his superiors that he also took *le Coeur Bleu* from Jean Philippe."

Hunter jumped to his feet. "He got a promotion for killing Jean Philippe?" Bile rose in his throat. "Dammit, why didn't you tell me this before?"

"I thought you knew. Hunter, calm down."

"Calm down? You tell me that Dietrich murdered my best friend, and I'm to calm down? I'll kill the bastard." He grabbed his gun from his knapsack and headed to the door. Madeleine tugged on his arm.

"Hunter, stop! You'll ruin all our plans." She planted herself in front of the door.

"To hell with the plans!" he shouted. "Get out of my way!"

"You'll have to drag me away. I won't move." She looked up at him defiantly. "How close do you think you can get to him before his guards shoot you? Even if you manage to kill him, you'll be killed or captured yourself when you try to escape."

"I don't care. Get out of my way!"

"No, I won't. If you don't care about yourself, think about the rest of us. Do you want to put us all in danger? Do you think Jean Philippe would want you to squander this chance to defeat the Nazis? Do you think he would want you to die so senselessly?"

That gave him pause. He stared into Madeleine's eyes, knowing she was right.

Carefully, he handed her the gun, and she set it on the table. He lowered his head, his fists clenching at his sides as his heartbeat gradually returned to normal. Even if he managed to shoot Dietrich he'd be killed instantly, and then they'd come after Madeleine, believing she was his wife. The thought that he'd come so close to putting her in danger shamed him.

Eventually he returned to the table and sat down. Madeleine poured him a glass of wine, and he downed it in one gulp, wishing he had something stronger.

For a long time she watched him but said nothing. Her expression revealed little of her thoughts. Then she rose and began clearing the table.

"You're an interesting man, Hunter Smith," she said at last. She said nothing more, leaving Hunter to wonder how she really felt. He wouldn't blame her if she thought him rash and stupid. Sometimes he had trouble believing his stupidity himself.

One thing was certain. She now knew every vile secret of his life, and his every weakness. He could never hope to measure up to his best friend.

He could never hope for Madeleine to see him as anything but a poor substitute.

Chapter Seven

After Hunter helped Madeleine wash the dishes, they went over their plans once more. Scuttlebutt in the kitchen was that General Dietrich was driving south tomorrow, Thursday, to meet an important visitor and bring him back to the chateau by Saturday. From their meetings with Monsieur Gagnon, Hunter knew the important visitor must be the South African businessman Karlheinz Schmidt, and that the possibility of owning *le Coeur Bleu* was what drew him to the chateau.

If all went well, *le Coeur Bleu* would be out of the country before Schmidt arrived.

"Tomorrow we'll go to work as usual, so as to not arouse suspicion. Since we can't get past the guard posted at the door, the only way in is through the window. You'll slip into the office and unlock a window when the guard takes his usual ten-minute break. We'll leave here just after midnight, taking the back lanes to the chateau. Monsieur Gagnon has hidden bicycles in some thick woods just outside the chateau gates. Once we have the diamond, we'll use the bicycles to rendezvous with the plane."

"How long do you think it will take you to open the safe, remove the diamond, and get out?"

"It's hard to estimate exactly, but I believe no more than ten minutes."

He didn't tell her that picking a lock could be a time-consuming endeavor. If he'd lost his touch, or if the lock proved tricky, it could take hours—hours they didn't have. The general must have believed the safe impenetrable, to entrust it with the safekeeping of *le Coeur Bleu*.

Madeleine sighed. "Good. I'll be glad when this is over."

"Yeah, we both will." He wouldn't relax until the Lysander landed safely on English soil and he knew Madeleine was safe.

She yawned, covering her mouth with her hand. "It's getting late. We should get some sleep."

"Yeah, right. Sleep." Hunter inwardly groaned. As if it were possible to get a good night's sleep with Madeleine lying only a few steps away.

Last night had been an excruciating exercise in self-control. Her silhouette, illuminated by the oil lamp behind the sheet, tantalized and teased. She'd unbuttoned her blouse and pulled it from her shoulders, then unfastened her skirt, letting it slide to the floor in one fluid motion. It had been impossible to look away. When she reached behind her back to undo the clasps of her bra, he'd nearly exploded, his body aroused and hungry with need. She had no idea what she did to him, and he intended to keep it that way.

Tonight would be different. He wouldn't hang around waiting to be tortured.

"I need to take a walk," he said, getting to his feet.

"Now? It's past ten. The German patrols will be out."

"I'll be careful. I couldn't sleep right now. I'm too keyed up."

He could see Madeleine wanted to argue with him. Was she concerned for him? Or for the success of the mission? Deep inside, his hopeful heart prayed she felt something for him.

He forcefully quashed that hope. Wishing for things he could never have would only make him miserable.

"All right, if you must." Lines of worry marred her beautiful brow. She grasped his hand and held it tightly. "But please stay away from the main roads, and please, please, be careful."

"I will."

For a moment he was tempted to throw caution to the winds and pull her into his arms. Would she let him kiss her when it wasn't for show? Would she let him make love to her?

She doesn't want you. She wants Jean Philippe.

He pulled his hand from hers. "I won't be long. Goodnight."

Hunter grabbed his jacket from a hook near the door and slipped quietly from the cottage. After checking for patrols, he took off in a brisk walk. But he knew no matter how fast he moved he couldn't outrun the feelings that told him he was headed for heartache.

****

Where was he?

Madeleine tossed in her bed, unable to sleep. Hunter had been gone for nearly an hour, and with each passing minute she grew more and more afraid. Had he become disoriented in the dark and lost his way? Perhaps he'd tripped on the cobblestones and turned an ankle. Had he been picked up by a German patrol?

She moaned in misery. *God, please not that. Anything but that.* She couldn't face the prospect of losing another person she cared for.

And she did care for him. In three short days she'd gone from open antagonism to being worried sick about him. She couldn't say how or when exactly it had happened, only that it had. The more she knew about him, the more she cared.

Enough. She swung her legs to the floor and lit the lamp beside her bed. She couldn't stay here any longer while Hunter could be out there hurt and bleeding, or worse. She pushed that possibility from her mind as she reached for her clothes.

The door opened, its squeaky hinges signaling that someone had entered, and Madeleine recognized Hunter's form in the semidarkness as he tried to close the door quietly behind him. Relief brought instant tears to her eyes. She ran to him, throwing herself into his arms.

"*Merci, mon Dieu!* Thank God you're all right! You were gone so long I thought something terrible had happened to you."

He held her tight, crushing her to his chest, and kissing her hair. "Maddie, I'm sorry. I didn't mean to worry you. I just needed to walk, to get some air."

She beat her fist against his broad chest and then lifted her gaze to look deeply into his eyes. "Don't ever leave me like that again, Hunter. Promise me you'll never leave me."

His mouth opened slightly, his eyes widening in surprise. Then he took her face between his two big hands, his expression changing to something fierce and determined. "I promise, Maddie. I'll never leave you. Not as long as you want me."

He kissed her then, a kiss so infinitely tender that it brought fresh tears to her eyes. Madeleine sighed against his mouth, warmth spreading through her and making her limbs heavy. His hands slid down her body with slow, infinite care, as if savoring each curve through the thin flannel of her nightgown. She leaned against him, whether for support or just to be closer to him she wasn't sure. She only knew nothing had felt so good, so right, not since…

Not since Jean Philippe.

Her husband's beloved face flashed through her memory. She still loved him. Had she betrayed his memory by having feelings for Hunter?

Guilt had her taking a step away from Hunter. He immediately dropped his hands, and for a wild moment Madeleine wanted to walk back into his embrace and feel his hands caress her body once more.

But that wouldn't be fair to either of them.

"Go to bed, Madeleine." The harshness in Hunter's voice caused Madeleine to avert her eyes in shame. She'd encouraged his kisses and his sensuous caresses and then turned away from him.

"Hunter, I'm sorry."

"Don't worry about it." His voice gentled. "Just go to bed. Please."

She extinguished the coal oil lamp before slipping between the cold sheets of her tiny bed. Clothes rustled as Hunter undressed and climbed into his own equally cold, lonely bed.

"Goodnight," he said.

"Goodnight," Madeleine whispered.

She knew it would be anything but a good night. Tomorrow they faced many dangers as they put their plans into action. But it wasn't fear that would cause her to lose sleep. Knowing that Hunter was lying just a few feet away, wanting her as much as she wanted him, would keep her awake tonight.

****

The sound of rain beating against the windowpane woke Madeleine from a restless sleep. After dressing behind the improvised privacy screen and making sure Hunter had adequate time to do the same on the other side, Madeleine stoked the woodstove and put on the kettle to make rose hip tea for breakfast. While the kettle came to a boil, she hurried outside to the outhouse to relieve herself, then came back inside to wash up. As she ladled lukewarm water from the reservoir in the woodstove into the tin basin sitting on the washstand, Hunter went outside to use the facilities. Madeleine washed and dried her face and hands, then with a sigh prepared their small breakfast. When he returned, his hair glistening with raindrops, he too washed up, then sat at the table, his eyes avoiding hers. They still hadn't said a word to each other, and the tension was unbearable. Madeleine could stand it no longer.

"Hunter, I'm sorry about last night. I shouldn't have—"

"Please, don't." He set down his cup and reached out to her, and for a moment Madeleine thought he would touch her. But instead he drew back his hand, wrapping it around his cup once more. "You have nothing to apologize for. I understand perfectly. If anyone should apologize, it should be me. I shouldn't have worried you by being away so long."

She nodded, surprised by the tears that clogged her throat and prevented her from speaking.

"I know you loved Jean Philippe," he said quietly. "He was a good man, the best. You don't easily forget a man like him."

She looked into Hunter's eyes. Although he appeared calm, she felt his sadness, his guilt. He'd loved Jean Philippe too. The death of his childhood friend had hit him hard, and he was suffering almost as much as she was. But last night she'd complicated things even further, making him feel guilty for wanting her. She'd wanted him, too, but her own guilt had stood in her way.

"Eat your breakfast, Madeleine. It's going to be a long day. You'll need all the strength you can get."

Madeleine nodded again and took a bite of her cheese. She stared at her plate, wondering if they'd live long enough to have this conversation again.

****

Madeleine watched from the safety of a doorway as the soldier guarding the door of the office looked both ways and then hurried toward the toilet. The man's bowels worked like precision German clockwork.

She checked the hallway herself before slipping out of her hiding place and making her way to the office. Her hand trembled slightly as she put the housekeeping key in the lock and turned the knob. The mechanism clicked quietly open. Madeleine opened the door just wide enough to slip inside and then closed the door softly behind her.

"Well, well, well. If it isn't the newly wed, newly pregnant Madame Lemay."

Madeleine nearly dropped the cleaning supplies she'd brought with her. Her voice shook almost as much as her hands. "General Dietrich. I didn't know you would be here.

Madame Beauchamp said you were on a business trip."

He pushed the elegant leather chair away from the desk and stood. "So you thought it would be safe to polish the desk in my absence."

"I do not wish to disturb you, sir." Madeleine pressed herself against the door, one hand on the doorknob in preparation for flight.

"You disturb me very much, madame." He walked around the desk. "I trust the pregnancy is going well?"

"Yes, very well. Except for the morning sickness," she added hastily.

The general looked her up and down. "It is unfortunate you are ill so often. No one would know just by looking at you. In fact, judging by your flat stomach, no one would guess you were pregnant at all."

"It's early days, sir. Only three months. It is too early for me to show." She squeezed the doorknob.

He advanced on her, coming to stand only inches away. Though he didn't lay a finger on her this time, his presence, so near and so menacing, caused her limbs to tremble in fear.

"It would be a shame if something were to happen to the baby," he said, a slight smile curling his lip. "Or to your husband."

Madeleine could only stare at him, frozen in terror. He would do it, too, she was sure. He would kill Hunter, or have him killed. And if there were a child, the general would destroy him, too.

He suddenly laughed and turned away. "Take your things and go away, Madame Lemay. You can do your polishing another time. I have work to do."

"Yes, sir."

Madeleine opened the door with shaking hands and hurried down the hall, her heart racing. She barely made it outside before her stomach revolted and she was sick in the rose bushes.

The rain beat down on her, soaking her to the skin and

cleaning the roses, washing away all traces that she'd been sick. She wished she could wash away her encounter with the general as easily.

After a few deep breaths, she straightened her back and slipped inside the chateau, careful to avoid the guard who was now at his post in front of the office once more. She took the back stairs to a washroom, where she rinsed her mouth and dried her hair with a towel as much as possible. She hardly recognized herself in the bathroom mirror. Her hair had begun to curl in wild waves around her face. Her pale skin made her appear ill and weak, but her eyes were the worst. They held a haunted quality, like a deer that knows the hunter's arrow is headed for its heart.

She pushed away from the sink. She couldn't fall apart now. With one last rub at the moisture in her hair, she left the washroom. She had to find Hunter.

Madeleine avoided the kitchen, knowing Madame Beauchamp would be there and would want to know why she hadn't finished her duties. Pulling back the curtain on the window of a side door used by the staff, she stared at the driving rain pelting a newly planted flowerbed, the tender plants drooping against the onslaught. The gardeners couldn't possibly be working outdoors in weather like this. They had to be in one of the outbuildings, a shed or perhaps the greenhouse. She grabbed an umbrella from the stand near the door and headed outside, bracing herself against the cold rain.

She searched two sheds before she found the gardeners working in the greenhouse, transplanting small seedlings into larger pots that would eventually be set out into the chateau's many flowerbeds. Madeleine nearly fainted with relief when she saw Hunter. As she approached him, he looked up, his surprise at seeing her evident on his face. The head gardener intercepted her before she could reach him.

"What are you doing here, madame?" he asked.

Madeleine gave him her best smile. "I just need to

speak to my husband for a moment. I promise I won't take him away from his work for long."

"All right," he said grudgingly, "but just for a moment. He's got work to do."

She folded her umbrella and hurried toward Hunter, who was working at the far end of the greenhouse. He walked toward her, meeting her halfway.

"I need to talk to you," she said.

"Madeleine, you're soaked." He grasped her arms, covered only by her light blouse. "You're cold." He rubbed his hands up and down her arms, lending her his warmth. "What's happened? Why are you here?"

"The general is still here," she whispered. "He didn't leave for the south after all."

Hunter went still, his hands grasping her elbows. "Did you see him?"

"Y—yes." The adrenaline rush subsided, leaving her to feel the full force of the cold and damp.

"What did he do to you?"

Hunter's eyes bore into hers, dark and forbidding. "Nothing. He didn't touch me."

"Then what did he say to you?" He gave her a gentle shake when she didn't answer. "Madeleine! Tell me!"

"I don't think he believes our pregnancy story. And he threatened you. Hunter, you're not safe here."

"Neither are you." He glanced over her shoulder. "They're watching us. Kiss me."

"What?"

"Kiss me like a wife madly in love with her husband."

His expression gave no hint of his feelings. Madeleine's heart rate accelerated as she stared into his eyes. She stepped into his embrace.

Hunter's arms closed around her, trapping her in a cocoon of warmth. His lips sought hers, tentative at first, and then when she opened her mouth and touched her tongue to his lips, he moaned, deepening the kiss, his tongue mating with hers. She pushed herself closer and felt his arousal against her belly. Madeleine's hand clutched at his jacket, his shirt. She wanted to feel his skin against hers, wanted him inside her…

The hoots and catcalls of the other gardeners brought them both back to the present. Hunter broke the kiss, loosening his hold and putting a bit of distance between them, though his arms still held her. The look on his face told Madeleine that the kiss had shaken him as much as it had shaken her. She'd never lost control in public like that before. She'd loved Jean Philippe with all her heart, but he had never made her want to strip off all her clothes and have sex in front of anyone who cared to watch. God help her, if Hunter hadn't stopped, she wouldn't have had the strength.

Madeleine's breathing finally returned to some semblance of normal, and her heart rate slowed. "What do we do?"

He kissed the end of her nose. "For now we go back to work, as if it is any ordinary day. We will talk tonight when we get home."

"All right." She found herself reluctant to leave him.

"Stay close to the other staff. Don't go anywhere alone."

"I won't."

He drew her into his arms for one last tender kiss before gently pushing her away.

"Go."

She nodded slightly and turned to leave, the gardeners giving her sly winks as she passed. At the exit, she opened her umbrella and took one final glance at Hunter. He was watching her intently, and for a moment Madeleine fought the urge to run back into his arms and never let him go.

Her world had just changed. Nothing in her life would be as it was. But for now she simply had to carry on as if the foundations of her being had not been shattered, as if she had not just realized she'd found the greatest love of her life. She slowly turned to face the rain once more.

Chapter Eight

Monsieur Gagnon poured wine for his guests while his wife busied herself putting food on the table for her husband, for Madeleine and Hunter, and for Michel, Anne Marie, and Gerard, three other local members of the Resistance. Their role was to provide backup fire power in the event Hunter and Madeleine were pursued by the Germans. They would delay the Germans long enough for them to reach the plane and take off. Of course it was probable that, if these Resistance fighters were forced to engage in a firefight, they would be killed. Hunter reached for his wine and took a sip, allowing himself this one glass. He'd need a clear head for his work tonight.

"What do you think it means that General Dietrich stayed at the chateau rather than driving south to meet Schmidt?" Madeleine asked Monsieur Gagnon.

"It could mean one of many things," he said with an eloquent Gallic shrug. "Perhaps the South African has changed his mind about purchasing the diamond. Or it could simply mean he will find his own way to the chateau."

"I think the exchange of the diamond for the iron ore is still set to happen," Michel said. "We have reports that some German army bigwigs from Berlin are headed for Lille in the next few days."

"It sounds like General Dietrich plans to have a little celebration," Hunter said.

Monsieur Gagnon nodded. "There is nothing the general would enjoy more than to take credit for making the biggest deal of the war. He has ambitions to rise to the top ranks of the Nazi party."

"We have to make sure that doesn't happen." Hunter would take great pleasure in bringing the arrogant bastard down, but he'd love even more to put a bullet in his brain. When he thought of what Dietrich had done to Jean Philippe and to Madeleine, his heart filled with a hot, burning hatred that threatened to rage into a conflagration he couldn't control.

He glanced at Madeleine and saw her looking at him as if she read his mind.

"We will," she said quietly. "He will pay, one way or the other."

"So we are agreed, then," Monsieur Gagnon said. "Hunter and Madeleine will complete the mission tonight, with Michel, Gerard, and Anne Marie providing assistance."

They all nodded their assent and then silently ate the simple meal Madame Gagnon had prepared. Hunter hoped it wouldn't be his last.

After they'd eaten their fill, Monsieur Gagnon produced a hand-drawn map showing the exterior walls and entrances of the chateau along with the grounds and the woods beyond. He pointed to the window of the general's office.

"Since Madeleine was unable to unlock the office window, and the twenty-four-hour guard at the door means we can't get in that way, we have no choice but to break a window to gain entry." He handed Hunter a small glass-cutting tool. "It will have to be done quietly so as not to alert the guard at the door or any of the soldiers patrolling the grounds."

Hunter examined the tool Monsieur Gagnon had given him. He could use it to make a circular hole just big enough for his hand to fit through and open the lock. But it would require time—time they didn't have. Every extra second meant their escape would be that much more difficult.

And that much more dangerous.

"Gerard will remain with me. If I receive any radio messages from England, he will relay them to you at the chateau. The rest of you will watch from the cover of the trees. If Monsieur Lemay gets into trouble, and the opportunity presents itself, you can start some sort of diversion to deflect the Nazis' attention from him. But if he is caught, I want no heroics to save him. You are to use your guns only if it is a matter of your own life or death. Gunfire will attract more soldiers and bring the wrath of the Nazis down on our heads. Our cell must survive." He turned to Hunter. "I'm sorry, Monsieur Lemay."

Hunter nodded. He understood. The group was more important than any one member.

He glanced toward Madeleine. She'd gone pale, her face drawn. He reached over and clasped her hand, and she looked up at him, giving him a tremulous smile.

Monsieur Gagnon continued. "Once the diamond is secured, Monsieur Lemay will make his way out of the chateau. The rest of you will escort Lemay and Madeleine to the rendezvous point with the plane, using the bicycles we have hidden in the woods. When they have left, you will return to your homes as if nothing has happened."

It sounded so simple. But Hunter knew that at any point the plan could go spectacularly wrong. He also knew that at any point he could die.

He had no desire to die. In fact, he had every wish to live. He glanced at Madeleine and saw she again watched him. He would do whatever he could to come back alive to her, and would take whatever little piece of her heart she was able to give him.

****

Madeleine packed a few clothes and everything that was precious to her in her knapsack. She took the puzzle box and the little box containing Jean Pierre's watch from her jewelry case and, wrapping them inside some clothes, placed them carefully inside the knapsack. She looked around the little cottage that had been her home for the last two months, since she'd come to Lille. The cottage had provided not only shelter from the elements but so much more. When she'd been frightened or sad, this place had been her refuge. It had become her home, and she would miss it.

She glanced at Hunter as he loaded his handgun, his face set in lines of determination. Would her next home be with him? Did she want it to be?

Hunter's kisses ignited fires inside her she'd thought long dead. He made her feel things she'd never felt before. Did she want more than just his kisses? Did she want a life with him?

Was it madness to consider spending her life with a man she'd known for all of four days? Perhaps it was, but in war, four days could be a lifetime.

Hunter looked up from his gun, sensing her gaze. "Are you all packed?"

"Yes." Madeleine patted her knapsack. "I've got everything I need here."

"Come, sit down." He pulled out the other chair. "You look sad. Are you all right?"

She had no idea. "Not sad, just…unsettled. I was thinking about how this will be the last evening for me in this little cottage, and in France. I can't imagine what life in England will be like. I don't even speak English!"

"You'll be fine. I'll make sure of it." He tucked his gun into the holster at his waist, hidden by his clothes, then pulled a watch from his pocket.

"Eleven p.m. We go soon." A flash of lightning illuminated the room with a brilliant display of power. The crash of thunder that immediately followed caused the cottage to shake.

"The storm's getting worse," Madeleine said. "It's going to make things much more difficult, isn't it?"

"Yes, it is. But on the other hand, the sounds of the storm will drown out any noise we might make." He took her hand. "It will be all right, Maddie. I promise."

She squeezed his fingers. Somehow she believed him.

Whatever happened, everything would be all right. As long as he was with her.

"I know it will."

"Good girl." He lowered his gaze to watch their joined hands. "You know, I told you practically my whole life story, but I know almost nothing of your background, or your family."

"There's nothing much to tell. I'm an ordinary girl, from an ordinary family, not like you, an ambassador's son."

His mouth twisted. "Trust me, the only thing extraordinary about my family was how much my parents disliked each other and how little they wanted to be parents to me. I'd much rather hear about your family."

Madeleine's heart broke at the thought of Hunter as a lonely, sad little boy with parents who gave him so little affection or attention. No wonder he had gravitated toward Hélène Bertrand. Jean Philippe had told her it was his mother who tucked Hunter in at night and nursed his childhood hurts.

"We lived in a little town not far from Paris. When my father died in an accident, my mother and I moved to Paris, where she got a job as seamstress. She was very talented and creative, and soon she was designing a line of ladies' clothing. She bought a little shop where wealthy women came for one-of-a-kind dresses from her. We lived in the apartment above the shop. I remember being very happy there."

"Is she still there, in the shop in Paris?"

"No. She died when I was nineteen. I still miss her every day. What about your parents? Are they still alive?"

"Yes, as far as I know. They moved to Georgetown, in Washington, D.C., last I heard. I haven't seen them in over two years. When they heard about my arrest, they washed their hands of me."

He tried to hide the pain of that abandonment, but Madeleine could plainly see the deep scars it had left.

He grinned at her. "We're supposed to be talking about you. How did you meet JP?"

"He arrested me."

"What?"

Madeleine laughed at his reaction. "After my mother died, I had no money, so I had to sell the shop. My intention was to sell only the building, not the contents, which included many of my mother's designs and, more importantly, the patterns. I made arrangements to store these items at the shop after the sale until I found another apartment. But the man who bought the shop reneged on our agreement. He refused to give me back my property, and then I found he had even sold some of the patterns. I was furious."

"What did you do?"

"I went to the shop and sat in the middle of the floor and refused to leave until he gave my property back to me. I had alerted the newspapers before I staged my little coup, and there were reporters everywhere. The new owner of the shop called the police, and Jean Philippe came to arrest me for trespassing."

"And he fell madly in love with you at first sight?"

"Not quite. I kicked him in the shins when he tried to haul me out of the shop. Perhaps it was love at second or third sight. For both of us. When we got to the police station, he gave me the name of a friend who was a lawyer. His friend helped me to successfully sue the new owner of the shop, and I got back my property. Jean Philippe and I married just a few weeks after we first met."

"That sounds like JP. He'd knock me to the ground for doing something stupid, then offer a hand up and help me fix whatever I'd done wrong. He was the most honorable, generous person I've ever known."

"Yes, he was a wonderful man." Madeleine fingered the delicate chain of the gold locket around her neck, remembering the love they'd shared. But Jean Philippe was dead. Perhaps it was time to let him go.

"He must have loved you very much, to give you that necklace. His father gave it to his mother as a wedding present. It meant the world to her."

"Yes, he told me that." The necklace had meant the world to her, as well. Jean Philippe had given it to her on their wedding day, a symbol of his love and commitment. The feel of it around her neck had comforted her after his death and in the lonely days that followed. Wearing the necklace made her feel that Jean Philippe was close to her somehow.

Hunter released her hand and again checked his watch. "We should get ready to go. We meet the others at the rendezvous point at midnight."

Her stomach fluttered nervously. She closed her eyes a moment and took a deep breath before nodding. "Yes, we should go."

"It'll be all right, Madeleine. I promise."

She smiled at him. They both knew he might not be able to keep such a promise, but still, somehow, she believed him.

****

The rain beat on Madeleine's face as she sat hunched in the bushes with Anne Marie and Michel. Despite the cape she wore, a cold trickle of rain inched down her back, chilling her to the bone. Her leather shoes were soaked through and caked with mud that felt more like a casing of ice.

But her physical discomfort was nothing compared to her fear at watching Hunter run stealthily between clumps of bushes and trees as he made his way toward the chateau. She breathed a sigh of relief when he reached the relative safety of the thick bushes under the windows of the office.

Her relief was short lived. Beside her, Anne Marie gasped, then quickly stifled the sound.

A German guard rounded the far corner of the chateau.

His path would take him directly past the office windows, mere feet from where Hunter hid. Madeleine prayed he'd seen the approach of the guard and would remain in his hiding place.

The guard used his flashlight to illuminate the ground in front of him, flashing it from side to side occasionally. When he was directly in front of the office windows, he flashed a beam of light on the windows and then over the bushes beneath. Madeleine held her breath. After a moment that felt like an eternity, he moved on.

Madeleine sighed in relief. Hunter's head popped up from the rhododendrons as he prepared to cut the glass.

A birdcall sounded just behind them. Gerard's signal. Michel gave the answering birdcall, and a moment later Gerard crawled toward them.

"The mission is aborted," he blurted. "The weather over the Channel is too difficult for the plane. It had to return to England."

"If Monsieur Lemay cuts the window they will know an attempt has been made on the diamond," Michel said.

"Why don't we go ahead and take the diamond," Anne Marie argued. "We can hide it until a plane can land and we can get it out of the country."

"If we take that stone without any means of escape, the Germans won't stop until they have it back. By the time they find it, we'll all be dead."

"We must stop Lemay," Gerard said.

For a second no one moved, everyone paralyzed in fear and indecision. Then Madeleine got to her feet and quickly checked for German patrols. "I'll go."

She took off before anyone could stop her. She had to get to Hunter, had to stop him. Rather than the circuitous route through the bushes that Hunter had taken, she cut straight across the lawn from her hiding place to Hunter's rhododendrons. Fear gave wings to her cold, sodden feet.

Hunter had already reached forward, ready to make the

cut in the window glass, when she arrived.

"No, stop!"

The glass-cutting tool fell from Hunter's hand as he whirled to face her. "What the hell are you doing here?"

"The mission is aborted. The plane cannot reach France tonight."

"All right. Let's get out of here."

A beam of light snaked along the ground a few feet away from where they stood. Hunter pushed Madeleine beneath the bushes, covering her with his body, but she could see the tool Hunter had dropped—it lay exposed on top of the wood chips and mulch the gardeners had spread under the rhododendrons. The mulch prevented muddy footprints from being detected, but it allowed the tool to be easily seen.

Madeleine held her breath as the light from the guard's flashlight washed over the chateau wall and along the thick bushes. She felt Hunter's hand move to his gun. She knew he would kill, if he had to, but only as a last resort.

At last the beam of light moved slowly along the side of the chateau until Madeleine could no longer see it. Hunter carefully moved off her, daring a peek between the thick bushes to check for guards.

"Are you all right?" he asked.

"Yes, I'm fine."

He picked up the glass cutter and offered his free hand to Madeleine. "Then let's go."

He pulled her to her feet, and with one quick look in either direction they dashed across the lawn to the safety of the trees. No one said a word as they made their way through the woods to the little-used side road where they'd stashed the bicycles.

"Do you want to take the bicycles?" Michel asked.

"No. Leave them. We'll need them tomorrow."

Madeleine groaned at the thought of doing this again tomorrow night. It had taken every ounce of courage she possessed to come out here tonight. The thought of starting all over again tomorrow terrified her.

Hunter glanced at her.

"Are you okay?"

She swallowed. "Yes. Fine."

He took her hand. "Let's go home."

Madeleine and Hunter split from the rest of the group, taking back streets and alleys to return to her cottage. She pushed open the door with trembling hands numb with cold. Hunter swept in behind her and closed the door, taking her knapsack from her back and setting it on the floor next to his.

"I'll get a fire started."

Now they were safe, the realization of what could have happened hit hard. The guards could have found them hiding in the bushes. They could have been shot on sight or perhaps questioned and tortured. Collette had been tortured before she was killed. She'd had cigarette burns on her breasts, and her fingernails had been removed.

Madeleine started to shake, her teeth chattering and her body trembling uncontrollably.

"Maddie?" Hunter took her hands in his. "You're freezing. Let's get you out of these wet clothes."

He pulled off her rain cape and made her sit so he could take off her wet shoes and socks. He laid them close to the woodstove to dry.

"We need some towels."

He brought a couple of thin towels from the hook next to the wash basin and began drying her hair. Once he got the worst of the moisture from her hair, he used the other towel to wipe her face with infinite gentleness, as if afraid she might break. He did the same with her feet and bare legs, holding her feet between his hands and gently rubbing to bring back the circulation. His tender ministrations brought tears to her eyes.

She loved him. No matter what he said about Jean

Philippe being the better man, she knew it wasn't true. Jean Philippe had once told her that Hunter was true and loyal and honorable but just didn't know it.

Madeleine knew he was all that and more. The fact that he had grown into such a loving man was made more remarkable by the loveless way he'd been raised.

"Maddie, the rest of your clothes are wet. I'll string up the sheet so you can change out of them and into something warm and dry."

"No."

"No? What do you mean? You need to get out of your wet clothes."

"I mean no, don't string up the sheet." She unfastened the buttons on her blouse with shaking hands, her eyes steady on his. "Make love to me, Hunter. Please."

He trapped her hands with one of his. "Maddie, you don't mean that. You've had a terrible shock, and you're upset. If you slept with me, made love with me, you'd regret it in the morning."

She shook her head. "No, you're wrong. I'd never regret making love with you. The only thing I'd regret is letting this time together pass us by. We may never have another chance."

She kissed his lips and looked into his eyes. She wanted to tell him she loved him, but would he believe her? She could scarcely believe it herself after so short a time. Yet in her heart she knew her love was solid and true and forever. However long forever might be.

"You're sure?" Hunter's dark eyes were wary, as if afraid she would change her mind. Madeleine sought to reassure him in the only way she knew how. She pushed her blouse off her shoulders, letting it fall to the floor. Then she unzipped her skirt and let it fall, as well. She stood before him wearing only her simple bra and panties. She unhooked the bra and let it drop.

"Yes, I'm very sure."

For a moment Hunter stood completely still, staring at her and saying nothing. Doubt crept into her mind. Had she misread him?

Madeleine lowered her head, embarrassed, raising her arms to fold them across her breasts. Hunter touched her arm, preventing her from covering herself.

"Don't. You're so beautiful. I can't believe...I can't believe you want me."

The vulnerability in his expression brought tears to her eyes.

"I do. Very much."

Hunter groaned and pulled her close, his mouth seeking hers, his hands caressing, kneading, possessing. She clutched at his broad shoulders, pressing herself tighter against him, wanting to feel his skin against hers. She shivered at the feel of his wet clothing against her bare skin. He'd been so concerned about her discomfort that he'd forgotten his own.

It only made her love him more.

She kissed his neck and then began unbuttoning his shirt. "You're soaked. You must be cold."

He ran his hands up and down her arms. "I hadn't noticed."

Madeleine smiled as he shrugged out of his wet shirt. She turned her attention to his trousers, unbuttoning the waistband and slowly pushing down the zipper. His penis strained against the fabric, and she stroked him, wanting to feel him in her hand, inside her body.

"God, Maddie. I need you."

"I need you, too," she whispered.

His mouth met hers, their tongues mating. He broke the kiss to place warm, wet kisses down her neck, her chest, her breasts. He took a nipple into his mouth, his tongue swirling, his teeth nipping gently. Madeleine's knees went weak at the sensation, and she clung to him for support. He went on his knees in front of her, kissing her stomach and lower abdomen. He tugged her panties down her legs, letting them pool at her feet, before placing a gentle kiss at the apex of her thighs. Her body quivered with need.

"Hunter, please. *Chéri*, please."

His big hands gripped her buttocks, bringing her closer. His tongue touched her most sensitive spot. Madeleine arched her back, gripping his shoulder. Hunter gently sucked and licked, building her desire, until she screamed out her release. Nothing had ever felt so exquisite. She slid to her knees, holding him and crying at the sheer beauty of it.

Hunter held her, whispering words of reassurance. There was only the two of them; nothing else in the world existed. She loved him forever and always.

Then he lifted her in his arms and laid her on the narrow bed. He stripped off his pants, never taking his eyes from hers. He stood in front of her, his body strong and beautiful, his erection hard and ready. Still, uncertainty shone in his eyes.

"Madeleine, it's been so long for me. I don't know how long…I don't want to disappoint you."

"You could never disappoint me." She held out her hand. "It's been a long time for me, too. Please, Hunter."

He took her hand and, when she tugged on it, straddled her on the bed. His kissed her, teasing her mouth open with his tongue. Her hands skimmed his body, touching, caressing, memorizing each hard muscle, the surprising softness of his skin, the wet silkiness of his hair. She welcomed his weight on her, reveled in the touch of his erection against her stomach. She lifted her hips and he entered her easily, letting out a cry of triumph.

"Madeleine!"

He pushed into her, filling her, stretching. The feeling was like nothing she'd experienced before. Madeleine arched her back, lifting her hips to reach him, matching her rhythm to his. They clung to each other, their breathing in perfect synchronization, their bodies pounding into each other in a frenzy of need. Wildness gripped her, pushing her to the edge of sanity.

Harder, faster, their bodies slicked with sweat.

Madeleine teetered on the edge of release once more, desire burning in her veins. Hunter took her breast into his mouth, sending her over the edge.

A moment later he found his own release, shouting her name. He collapsed on top of her, their bodies still joined. She held him, wanting to hold him forever.

No matter what happened tomorrow, she'd never let him go.

Chapter Nine

Bright sunshine streaming through the windows woke Hunter the next morning. He blinked, unable for a moment to orient himself. Then he saw Madeleine curled next to him, her hand resting on his chest. Memories of the night flooded back. She'd been liquid fire in his arms, her heat branding his body and his heart and making him hers.

He knew now what love was. He'd thought he was in love with Natasha, but his feelings for her paled in comparison with the torrent of emotion he felt for Madeleine. Nothing compared with the way he felt for her. He loved her so much it frightened him.

But what frightened him more was that he had no real idea what she felt for him. Had she believed herself so close to death that she simply wanted to feel alive by making love with him?

He prayed her feelings ran deeper than that. He wanted to spend the rest of his life with her. He wanted to love her, and be loved in return, in whatever time they were given.

Madeleine's eyes fluttered open, and after a moment they focused on his face. She smiled, her face more radiant then the sun bursting into the tiny cottage.

"Good morning." She lifted her hand to touch his unshaven face. He brushed her hair from her forehead.

"Good morning."

"Did you sleep well?"

"Yes, very well. Not long, but well."

"I know. I feel the same way. I wish we could simply stay here all day and for once forget about the war and the Nazis. For one day I'd like to tune out the world and stay here with you." She snuggled a little closer, laying her head on his chest. Hunter ran his hands through her hair, enjoying the way the silky strands slid between his fingers.

"There's nothing I'd rather do than spend the day in bed with you," he said regretfully. "But we have to go to work as if nothing has happened. Or is going to happen."

Madeleine sat up, wrapping the sheet around herself, her expression resigned. "Yes, I know. I'll start the fire."

He stopped her when she started to leave the bed. "Wait."

Hunter tugged at the sheet, pulling it away to reveal the beauty of Madeleine's naked body. Her breasts were exquisite, so full and lush, their shape perfectly round. Dark hair tumbled down her back in a riot of curls that begged to be touched. Pale skin shimmered in the morning light. He drank it all in, imprinting her in his memory. Whatever happened in the next few hours, in the next few days, he would always remember her this way.

"Someday," he said, touching her hair, "we'll have that day in bed. I promise."

****

As Madeleine finished mopping the kitchen floor, Madame Beauchamp appeared in the doorway. "Madeleine, General Dietrich has requested that you make sure the guest rooms are aired and cleaned and ready to receive guests."

"*Oui*, madame. When do the guests arrive?"

"Tomorrow. The chateau must be all perfection. We must not displease the general."

"*Non,* madame. I will see to the guest rooms immediately."

"He has also asked that you polish and dust the furniture in his private office. He says he turned you away when you came to clean, but he wants it perfect in preparation for his guests."

Madeleine stared at the older woman. She'd tried so hard to avoid the general since yesterday, but here she was being thrown in his path. The thought of the general kissing her again, touching her, revolted her, especially now, after making love with Hunter. She belonged only to him, could imagine herself only with him.

Yet being asked to clean the room was the perfect excuse, and the perfect opportunity, to unlock the window. They'd need every advantage if their mission was to succeed tonight.

Her distress and indecision must have shown on her face. Madame Beauchamp touched her arm.

"I know that right now he is in the ballroom with members of his staff. Go quickly to his office and do your work before he returns."

Madeleine nodded in relief. "*Oui,* madame. Thank you."

The older woman smiled briefly and squeezed her arm. "Be careful, my dear."

She nodded, grabbed her cleaning supplies, and hurried to the office. When she arrived, a guard she'd never seen before stood at attention outside the door. She lifted her mop and motioned toward the door.

"General Dietrich requested his office be cleaned and polished."

The guard looked her up and down, his blue eyes hard and cold. Madeleine stifled a shiver. The contempt she saw in his stare was not of a sexual nature, like the looks she'd so often received from General Dietrich. Instead, this young soldier's eyes reflected his infinite disdain for her as a human being. He thought himself superior to her because he was a man, a German, a soldier. She was nothing but a woman—far worse, she was French and a servant.

Somehow that made him much more dangerous.

She lowered her gaze in submission. This man expected nothing less.

At last he unlocked the door. "Go," he ordered in French, motioning with his gun. "Leave the door open."

She quickly stepped inside, aware of his eyes on her. Better to do what she needed to do right in front of him. Madeleine unlocked the window and threw it open.

"What are you doing?" the soldier asked, his gun poised and ready. Madeleine forced herself to look away from the gun.

"The general asked that all the rooms be aired after yesterday's rain."

"Fine. Make sure you close and lock the window before you leave."

"*Oui*, monsieur."

She got on with her work, quickly polishing and dusting every surface before mopping the floor. When she had finished, she closed the window, making a great show of locking it, knowing the young soldier watched her every move.

"I am done here," she said. She slowly gathered her cleaning supplies, racking her brains for a way to unlock the window without being detected. They couldn't have a repeat of last night. Cutting the glass would take too much time and could be too easily detected. Hunter needed to be able to get in, do his job, and get out as quickly as possible.

"*Schnell*! *Schnell*! Hurry! What is the matter with you, woman!"

Bastard. Madeleine contented herself with a quick thought of what she'd like to do to the arrogant pig.

An idea flashed into her mind, and with a sudden movement, she knocked over the bottle of vinegar and water she used to clean glass. The mixture quickly spread over the general's pristine desk.

"You clumsy cow!" the soldier bellowed. "Look what you've done!"

Madeleine dabbed ineffectually at the spill with her dusting cloth. "I need something to soak it up. Please, run to the bathroom and grab some towels."

"Me?" he said in disdain. "You made the mess. You

clean it up."

Madeleine leaned against the desk and let the vinegar and water soak into her skirt. "If I move, this mess will spill all over the general's rug and it will smell of vinegar for days. He'll blame you as much as he'll blame me."

She could read the indecision in his eyes. He didn't like leaving his post, but he liked inviting the wrath of his commander even less. He disappeared out the door, boots echoing on the marble floor as he ran down the hall.

Madeleine ran to the window, flipped the lock, and returned to her spot at the desk without a drop of vinegar falling onto the rug beneath the desk. She sighed in relief. A moment later the soldier returned with the towels, and she wordlessly cleaned up the mess. After giving the desk another quick coat of wax and placing a couple of drops of lavender oil in an ashtray to chase away the smell of vinegar, she hastily left. She prayed the soldier wouldn't open the window for fresh air and realize she had again unlatched the lock.

She also prayed the man she loved would be safe tonight.

****

The ground in their hiding place under the trees was still wet from yesterday's deluge, but at least it wasn't raining on their heads tonight. They watched a guard sweep his flashlight beam over the chateau walls and grounds. Hunter timed them; the guards made their rounds in ten-minute intervals. He'd have to be very quick and damn near invisible.

"All right, same scenario as last night. I make my way to the window and hide under the bushes. When I'm sure the coast is clear I open the window, which with any luck no one has locked since Madeleine was in the room this morning." He smiled at her. Her courage and resourcefulness never failed to amaze him. "Once I've got the diamond, I check the time and watch for guards making their rounds. I climb out the window again and close it. Hopefully no one will realize the diamond is gone until Madeleine and I are airborne and the rest of you are safely home in your beds."

"If a guard gets too close to you, we've prepared a diversion to distract him," Michel added.

"Good." Hunter knew he'd need all the help he could get. "If I don't make it out, I want the rest of you to get away from here as fast as you can." He reached for Madeleine's hand. "If I get caught—"

"No! Don't even talk that way! You won't get caught."

"Madeleine, listen to me. If I don't make it out, I want you to take that plane back to England."

She began shaking her head before he'd finished speaking. "No, I won't go without you."

"Madeleine, they think you're my wife. If I'm captured, you're the first person they're going to look for. Promise me you'll get on that plane."

"No, I won't promise you that." Her beautiful eyes welled with tears.

He grasped her upper arms and gave her a little shake, his voice a harsh whisper. "Madeleine, promise me. I can bear anything as long as I know you're safe. If General Dietrich got hold of you…"

He couldn't finish, but she understood. She gave a brief nod. "All right. I'll go."

"Okay. Good."

He pulled her close and kissed her. He'd meant for the kiss to be quick, but she gripped his jacket and clung to him, deepening the kiss. For a moment Hunter lost himself. He felt every emotion this woman evoked, every hope he had for a future together.

Too soon, he had to break the kiss and push away from her. He needed to concentrate on the job at hand. Michel looked at his watch. "The last guard just went by. You've got about eight minutes to get to the window and get inside."

"Okay." He slipped on his leather gloves. "Look after

her, Michel."

The young man nodded. *"Oui."*

Hunter clapped him on the back and, with one final look at Madeleine, ran across the lawn, darting between trees and bushes until he reached the chateau. He estimated he had enough time left to slip inside the office window, as long as it was still unlocked. He stretched to his full height. He was just tall enough to see inside the room, and at the moment it appeared deserted. He pushed upward on the window sash and prayed.

Please, please open.

His prayers were answered. The window easily and soundlessly slid open. Perhaps the rest of the mission would go just as smoothly.

Hunter used every ounce of strength he had to hoist himself up and through the window, landing with a small thud on the floor of the office. He held his breath, lying perfectly still. Had the guard posted outside the door heard him? When no one entered the room with guns blazing, he assumed he'd arrived undetected.

The beam of a flashlight outside on the lawn caught his attention. He quickly pushed the window sash down and dove under the desk. He cursed silently when he saw that the window remained open a sliver. Would the guard outside notice? From his hiding place under the desk he saw the flashlight throw eerie beams up and down the walls, like grasping fingers reaching out for him. At last the light disappeared, and he breathed a sigh of relief as he crawled out from under the desk.

Now came the hard part. The safe.

Hunter felt along the bookcase until he found the release mechanism that opened the secret compartment containing the safe. He applied pressure until he heard a slight pop. The bookcase swung open.

He took a deep breath and pulled a small flashlight from his pocket, taking his first close look at the safe. He'd never opened one like it before, but Gaston used to tell him he had a natural feel for the business of opening safes. Any lock would readily whisper its secrets to him. He hoped the old man was right.

He stuffed the flashlight back in his pocket and took out two thin, springy strips of metal which he inserted into the keyhole. Delicately he manipulated the metal strips, using one to exert a small turning force while the other felt the various pins and levers, lifting them inside the lock. Hunter waited for one of the pins to reach the right height, waited to feel that little give in the turning pick that signaled the lock was giving up its secrets.

He held his breath as he worked the picks. Soon the telltale tug on the turning pick let him know one of the pins had been raised. As long as the turning force was maintained, this pin would remain raised while the feeler pick worked on the next pin. But Hunter knew from experience how delicate and unpredictable picking a safe lock could be. More than once he'd made it all the way to the last pin only to have something slip, letting all the pins fall down like a row of dominoes. When that happened, there was nothing to do but start all over again.

Hunter concentrated on slowing his heartbeat and controlling his breathing so that he made no unintentional movements, even ones of minute proportion. His complete attention focused on the picks and the feel of them in his hands. Sometimes it seemed he could *see* the pins as they rose into place. The sensation was almost magical. He prayed he could experience that magic now.

One by one he felt the pins raise as he gently but firmly maintained pressure with the turning pick. Almost there, almost there…

A sudden urge to sneeze caught him unaware. He had no choice but to fling one arm across his nose and mouth to muffle the sound. He succeeded in muting the sneeze, but his action resulted in all the pins falling back. Hunter inhaled and began again.

One by one each pin rose again and took him closer to opening the safe. Finally, the last pin gave a tiny pull and the safe clicked open.

Hunter sent a word of thanks heavenward. He let out the breath he'd been holding, sighing in relief. Maybe this would really work.

Quickly he removed the picks from the lock and shone his flashlight inside the safe until he found a small box. He opened the lid and smiled. *Le Coeur Bleu* glowed blue fire in the flashlight's beam. He couldn't resist one quick look. Removing the diamond from the box, he took a jeweler's loupe from his pocket and examined the stone.

What the hell?

He'd never seen *le Coeur Bleu* before, but it was reported to have only one small flaw. The diamond in his hand had many flaws. And the color, while blue, was not the deep blue that one would expect from a fancy-grade diamond like *le Coeur Bleu*. He couldn't be sure without more testing, but the weight of the stone felt lighter then the thirty-five carats it should have been.

Hunter checked the safe once more. It was cluttered with papers, a gun, but no other jewelry boxes. He couldn't be sure of the diamond's authenticity from such a simple test, but it raised doubt in his mind. What should he do?

He stuck the box in his pocket. He had to take it. He could be totally wrong and the diamond perfectly legitimate. They'd sort it out later. But for now he had to get out of Dietrich's office.

Voices sounded on the other side of the office door. Hunter froze, listening. Did he close the safe and the bookcase and wait for them to leave, or should he make a dash for the window?

The choice was taken out of his hands. The door burst open and light flooded the room. General Dietrich entered, followed by his guard, who pointed his gun at Hunter.

Dietrich grinned.

"Well, well, if it isn't Monsieur Lemay. Does your wife know where you go when you leave her bed? She'll be cold and lonely and in need of company. Perhaps I can do something to remedy that."

Rage filled Hunter. He wanted to wipe the smug smile from the bastard's face. He'd gladly kill him with his bare hands. But he knew if he made a move he'd be shot on the spot. Another guard searched him and removed his gun.

Thank God Madeleine was leaving France tonight.

More people crowded into the small office. A large balding man with round glasses entered, followed by a woman in a fur coat. She was speaking to her companion as they crossed the threshold.

"Karl, darling, when can we see *le Coeur Bleu*? We've been travelling for days, and I'm so anxious to see it."

That voice, the accent. It couldn't be…

She gave an audible gasp. "*Mon Dieu*! Hunter? Hunter Smith?"

Hunter inclined his head. He should have known his luck wouldn't hold out.

"Natasha. It's been a long time."

****

From her hiding place in the trees, Madeleine concentrated on the window of the office, willing Hunter to climb out and come back to her. It was taking too long. Had something gone wrong?

Light suddenly glowed in the window and her heart lodged in her throat. She got to her feet. "I have to know what's going on."

Michel grabbed her arm. "No. You heard Monsieur Lemay. He wants us all to get out of here, and he wants you to get on that plane. There's nothing we can do for him now."

"No!" She struggled to control her tears. "I won't believe there's nothing we can do. We've got to help him!"

"It would be suicide to try to free him," Gerard said. "We are only four against dozens of Germans, perhaps hundreds."

"Madeleine, I'm sorry." Michel's voice was filled with regret. "He made me promise to get you on that plane, and that's what I intend to do."

"I need to know what's going on in that room." She grabbed Michel's arm. "I just need to know."

She knew Michel wanted only to protect her and the other members of their cell. But she'd be damned if she let another man she loved die without doing something to help him. She'd rather die herself.

"All right. But if you're not back here in five minutes, we're gone and you're on your own. We don't know you. Understood?"

"Yes." She scanned the lawn for patrols and then raced toward the chateau and the safety of the bushes beneath the window.

Oh, God! Hunter!

Forcefully pushing all anxiety and fear from her mind, she concentrated on listening. The window was open only a sliver, but she could make out voices.

"You know him?" A man's voice, in accented German, sounded agitated.

"We knew each other in London," a woman said. She spoke German with an accent Madeleine couldn't identify. "How nice to see you again, Hunter."

"Hunter?" The general's booming voice made Madeleine shiver. "Is that his real name?"

"Yes, Hunter Smith. Sometime jewel thief and full-time diamond broker. Son of the former American ambassador to France."

"American?" The general laughed. "Well, well, Monsieur Lemay, you are a man of many surprises. If you would be so good as to return the diamond to me..."

Madeleine's spirits fell even lower. Hunter's cover was

totally blown. Which meant that her cover as Madame Lemay was also blown.

"Natasha, I should have known you would be involved in this." Hunter spoke in excellent German. "I assume this gentleman is Herr Schmidt. Does he know about your husband?"

"Husband?" Obviously Natasha's husband was news to Herr Schmidt. "What is he talking about?"

"He's talking nonsense, darling. He blamed me when he was caught stealing a suite of jewels. He would say anything to save his skin." She gave a brittle laugh. "If you hadn't been so greedy, you might have gotten away with it, but you insisted on going back for the rest of the jewelry. Last I heard, you were in an English jail. How did you get out so quickly?"

"Time off for good behavior."

A prickle of doubt crept into Madeleine's thoughts. Hunter told her he'd been caught trying to return the jewels. Would Hunter lie to get into her bed?

"Take him away," ordered the general.

"Herr Schmidt, you might want to take a very close look at that diamond. The general is trying to stick you with a fake." Hunter spoke quickly, as if being rushed from the room.

"Wait! I want to hear what he has to say!"

"The man is lying. The diamond has been authenticated by experts."

"My ships are waiting off the coast of Africa for word from me. If I am not convinced of the diamond's authenticity, they will return to Cape Town with their cargo."

"I give you my word the diamond is real."

Herr Schmidt's voice was angry. "And I can assure you I need far more than your word. I have my own expert with me. He will make the determination."

"Lock him up," the general ordered. He sounded

furious. Hunter cried out as if he'd been struck, and Madeleine winced. Dear God, what was she to do?

For now, the only thing she could do was to get back to Michel and the others before they deserted her. Perhaps there was some way she could convince them to help her rescue Hunter.

She didn't let herself think about what might happen if she didn't succeed.

Chapter Ten

Michel insisted on leaving the chateau grounds immediately, despite Madeleine's pleas. She had no choice but to go with the others to the rendezvous spot with the Lysander. Her heart cried with each step that took her farther away from Hunter. But she was only one person. If the others wouldn't help her, there was little she could do for him on her own.

By the time they arrived at the rendezvous, another member of the cell was already there with a truck. Michel and Gerard hurried to place the torches that would mark the landing strip for the Lysander. They watched from a short distance away as the plane landed, then ran toward it to unload its precious cargo of arms.

In a few moments the plane was unloaded and the pilot called out in broken French, "We must leave."

Michel pushed Madeleine toward the plane. "Quickly! He's ready to go."

"No." Madeleine stood her ground. "I won't go. Not without Monsieur Lemay."

"I promised him you'd get on that plane. There's nothing you can do for him."

She shook her head. "I don't believe that. I'm staying."

"Where will you stay? You can't go back to your cottage. Now that they know your marriage to Monsieur Lemay is a sham, that's the first place they'll look for you. And you can't go to Monsieur Gagnon. You will put him and his wife and the whole operation in jeopardy."

Madeleine hesitated. Michel was right. By staying here, she put all the others in her cell in peril. As much as she wanted to believe she would remain loyal to her friends, no one could predict what she might reveal under torture.

"She can stay with me."

Madeleine blinked at Anne Marie as the young woman faced Michel defiantly. "I have a place I can hide her."

"Anne Marie, don't be a fool! It's too dangerous!"

"My sister died for that diamond! If we don't get it back, Collette's death will be for nothing!"

Madeleine stared at her. Anne Marie was Collette's sister? To protect their cell, they purposely learned very little about each other's private lives, but...her sister? Madeleine's heart went out to the girl.

"We must go!" the pilot called again.

"This is your last chance, Madeleine. Monsieur Lemay's wish was for you to go to England, to safety. Will you go?"

Madeleine was no hero. The thought that she might be captured and tortured terrified her. General Dietrich would take great delight in savaging her himself. But facing those horrors would be easier than fleeing to safety and knowing she'd let Hunter die.

She shook her head. "No. I'm staying."

Michel sighed. "All right. Stay. But don't expect any help. You're on your own." He glanced at Anne Marie. "Both of you."

He signaled the pilot to leave, and in a few moments the small plane disappeared. Without another word Michel and Gerard left, as well, taking their cache of rifles with them. Anne Marie turned to Madeleine.

"Come. We must go to my hiding place. Then we will plan Monsieur Lemay's escape."

Tears of gratitude flooded unexpectedly into Madeleine's eyes. Would she have as much strength and courage as this young woman to do what was necessary to free Hunter?

She brushed away the tears and picked up her knapsack.

"Yes. We must go and plan."

She prayed it wasn't already too late.

****

Anne Marie's hiding place was a root cellar dug into the side of a hill on a farm a couple of kilometers out of the city. The entrance was obscured by brush and tall grasses. If Anne Marie had not led her to the spot and pointed out the wooden door to the cellar, Madeleine would never have found it.

Using the dim moonlight to illuminate the room, the younger woman made her way inside. Madeleine followed her, and Anne Marie closed the entrance door, sealing them inside, before lighting a candle on a small wooden table. Madeleine looked around the tiny earthen room. Wooden beams supported the walls and ceiling. Empty glass jars were stacked on shelves lining three walls. A large wooden bin took up the fourth wall. The bin was probably used to store potatoes, but right now it was empty. Thinking of food made Madeleine's stomach growl. Anne Marie took a baguette from her knapsack and, after breaking off some for herself, offered it to Madeleine.

"Since the root cellar is empty, no one comes here."

Madeleine chewed gratefully on the stale bread, not sure when she might have her next meal. Everyone in France was hungry these days.

"How long have you been staying here?"

"Since Collette was killed. The Nazis knew we were sisters, so when they found out she was *Maquis* they came looking for me, as well."

"I'm sorry about Collette. She was very brave."

Anne Marie nodded. "She was brave, but she was also reckless. She deliberately sought a relationship with General Dietrich so she could learn more about the Nazis' movements. She took too many chances."

"If it weren't for her, we would know nothing about their plans for *le Coeur Bleu*."

"Yes, and now Monsieur Lemay is imprisoned, and you

and I are hiding here like a couple of rats."

"We can't let them have that diamond, Anne Marie."

"The diamond brings nothing but sorrow and death. It's already lost me my sister."

Madeleine reached across the table and grasped her hand in wordless support. She knew exactly how Anne Marie felt. The diamond had cost Jean Philippe his life and now threatened to destroy Hunter. The thought of losing him caused a physical ache in her chest. But she couldn't give in to the grief. Hunter's life depended on her.

"We must plan, Anne Marie. We have to think of some way to get Monsieur Lemay out of the chateau."

Anne Marie nodded, set the remainder of her baguette on the table, and got to her feet. Extracting a large envelope from its hiding place behind one of the shelves, she laid the contents of the envelope on the table.

"What is this?"

"These are maps Collette made of the inside of the chateau. She did a lot of exploring while she worked there, and she wrote everything down."

Anne Marie opened one of the folded papers and smoothed it out over the table. A pencil drawing of the chateau's first floor was revealed. Collette had marked the entrance to every room, the location of every closet and every window. Some lines colored in red drew Madeleine's attention. She pointed to one of them.

"What's this?"

"It's one of the secret passageways. They are located throughout the building, although some have been sealed off over the years. Collette explored as many of them as she could."

"Where do you think Monsieur Lemay would be held?" She refused to believe he was already dead.

Anne Marie unfolded another map. "Here." She pointed to the wine cellars beneath the chateau. "It would be the most logical place. There are no windows to escape from, and only one door in and out. Collette once told me that General Dietrich held a prisoner there for a few days before deporting him to the east."

Madeleine nodded, trying not to think that either fate, Collette's or that of the unfortunate prisoner, would also be Hunter's. "If there are no other doors, no windows, how could we get him out?"

"There's only one possibility." Anne Marie brought forward the first floor map once more and pointed to some red lines near the kitchen. "Collette found the entrance to a passageway behind a broom closet. She wasn't able to explore the passageway, but she felt certain it led directly to the wine cellars. One of the old-timers who had worked at the chateau for many years told her that in the old days when the owners held a dinner party, the servants would be sent up and down that passageway for wine."

Anne Marie shuffled the maps, setting on top one that showed the outside perimeter of the chateau, complete with all its entrances. She pointed to a part of the building farthest away from the kitchen.

"While you search the secret passageway and release Monsieur Lemay from the wine cellar, I will start a fire in the north wing as a diversion. The fire should keep the Germans too busy to notice what is going on in the kitchen."

She produced a key from her pocket and slipped it into Madeleine's hand. "Collette had this key to the kitchen door made, so she could enter the chateau undetected."

"Thank you." At least she had a way in. Getting out, with Hunter, would be up to her. Madeleine clutched the key in her hand. "So in theory there should be a passageway leading directly from the kitchen to the wine cellar."

"Yes, in theory. Assuming the passageway hasn't been closed off over the years."

"I guess I'll have to test that theory. It's the only chance I've got."

****

As prison cells went, the wine cellar had its advantages. The racks were filled with some of the finest wines France had to offer. General Dietrich certainly knew how to live the good life.

But even with its luxurious contents, the wine cellar remained a prison. No, Hunter amended, a living tomb. The cold stone walls pressed in on him, squeezing the life, and the will to live, from him. The constant darkness made him feel as if he were already dead. Perhaps he was.

He could expect no help from the Resistance. To attack the chateau would be futile and would only result in all their deaths and the destruction of the cell. He was utterly and completely alone.

The only thing that eased his despair was knowing that Madeleine was safely in England by now.

He dropped his head into his hands and groaned. *Madeleine.* He'd failed her, failed Jean Philippe. JP had given his life to keep *le Coeur Bleu* out of Nazi hands, and now his sacrifice was all for naught. That is, if the diamond in the general's possession was the real thing.

His gut told him the diamond he'd pulled from the general's safe was not *le Coeur Bleu.* He was reasonably sure it was a diamond, but its quality was far inferior to that of the famed Blue Heart. If that was the case, then where was the real Blue Heart? Was the general trying to take Herr Schmidt's iron ore while keeping the real diamond for himself? He'd have to know that Schmidt would want the authenticity of the diamond confirmed. Why would he take such a risk?

Unless he didn't know the diamond in his possession was not *le Coeur Bleu.*

Hunter slapped his hand against the cold, hard stone wall beside him. There was little he could do about the diamond as long as he was locked in this tomb.

A key rattled in the ancient lock, and the heavy wooden door creaked open. The one overhead light bulb flashed on, and Hunter shaded his eyes against the glare. Natasha entered his cell, still wearing her fur coat. She delicately sniffed the dank air.

"I hope the accommodations aren't too oppressive, darling." She spoke in English, probably so the guard standing just outside the door could not understand her.

"I guess the general keeps the more elegant rooms for paying customers." Inwardly he bristled at the term of endearment she used for him. He hadn't been her darling for a long time. In fact he doubted he ever had been.

"If the room isn't to your liking, perhaps I can help you secure more comfortable lodgings. Elsewhere."

"Just spit it out, Natasha. What do you want?"

"I want the diamond. The real one. Where is it?"

"I have no idea. Ask your friend the general."

She gave him an impatient glare. "Do you want more money? Is that it? All right, I'll give you fifty percent of the proceeds of the sale of the diamond. I already have a buyer lined up."

Hunter laughed. "Do you ever stop scheming? Aren't you supposed to be helping Herr Schmidt secure the diamond? What does your husband say of all your affairs? He must be an exceedingly tolerant man."

"He's also an exceedingly dead man," Natasha said. She turned her face away, but not before Hunter caught a flash of pain. Perhaps somewhere deep inside she still had a heart that bled.

"How did he die?"

"Herr Schmidt had him killed. He thought I was a little too close to my 'brother.' So you see, I owe little loyalty to the man."

"Yes, I see. But the problem is, I have no idea where the real diamond is, or if one even exists."

"I don't believe you."

Hunter shrugged his stiff shoulders and rubbed the one that had become sore from lying on the stone floor. "Why would I risk breaking into the chateau for a fake diamond? I thought it was the real Blue Heart, same as you. But perhaps we're getting ahead of ourselves. We don't know for sure that the diamond in the general's possession isn't *le Coeur Bleu*."

"I believe in you, darling." Natasha took a cigarette from a gold case and offered one to Hunter, which he declined. He took the lighter from her hand and held the flame to the end of her cigarette while Natasha inhaled deeply. "You know diamonds better than anyone I've ever known, with the possible exception of Herr Schmidt. If you have a feeling that this stone is not *le Coeur Bleu*, even after only a quick inspection, I tend to believe you."

Hunter grinned as he handed back her lighter. "I'm touched that you have so much faith in my abilities."

"Your abilities have been very useful in the past." She took another deep drag on her cigarette, exhaling a plume of smoke. "So do we have a deal? Where is the real diamond?"

"I already told you, Natasha. I don't know. And even if I did, I wouldn't tell you." Hunter paced the tiny room. "It was you, wasn't it? You sent Jean Philippe the telegram that he thought was from me. You contacted the Gestapo and had JP walk into a trap. Why? You didn't even know Jean Philippe."

"Because he had *le Coeur Bleu* and I wanted it." She inhaled deeply. "When I found the telegram he'd sent you, saying he had *le Coeur Bleu*, I knew I had to have it. But things didn't turn out the way I'd planned. My contact in Paris was ready to meet with him and take the diamond off his hands. I sent the telegram in your name because I knew your friend trusted you. But the Gestapo must have intercepted the telegram. My contact was killed and your friend was arrested. I had to resort to Plan B to obtain the diamond."

"Plan B is Herr Schmidt, I take it."

"You don't think I would consort with the man if it

wasn't for the diamond, do you?" She inhaled again. "I'll ask you one last time. Where is the Blue Heart?"

"I don't know." How could he have ever imagined himself in love with this woman? Why had he never seen how ruthless and mercenary she was?

She flicked the ash from her cigarette onto the stone floor, her mouth set in a hard line. "Fine. You're welcome to stay here, then. You'll never be one of them, you know. You'll never be the paragon of virtue your dear friend Jean Philippe was. You're more like me than you want to admit. You're a thief at heart. The sooner you admit it and quit trying to be something you're not, the happier you'll be. And the more alive you'll be."

She turned on her heel and rapped sharply on the wooden door; a guard opened it and let her out. The echo of the slamming door bounced off the stone walls, ringing in his ears, as the light above him went out.

Maybe she was right. Maybe his parents had been right, as well, when they'd disowned him saying he was nothing but a common thief and an embarrassment to the family. Hélène had been the only person who ever thought he was worth something. Hélène and Jean Philippe. Jean Philippe had trusted him with his life.

And he'd let him down.

Chapter Eleven

Anne Marie left their hideaway in time to reach Monsieur Gagnon's house and return before dawn. Monsieur Gagnon would use his radio to contact the British to send a plane. If all went well, Madeleine and Hunter would rendezvous with the Lysander and make their escape from France in less than twelve hours.

If all goes well. They'd been down this road before.

Madeleine rolled onto her back and flung an arm across her eyes, unable to escape into sleep. Her thoughts were filled with worries for Hunter. Was he really in the wine cellar? Had they beaten him? Was he still alive?

She shifted uncomfortably on her pallet of blankets on the dirt floor. She couldn't dwell on her last thought. He *had* to be alive.

With an effort, she focused her thoughts on other concerns. She remembered the conversation she'd overheard in General Dietrich's office while hiding beneath the window. Hunter had said the general was trying to sell Schmidt a fake diamond. Was that true? Had Hunter discovered the diamond in the general's possession was a fake? Or was he trying to seed doubt in Schmidt's mind? If the general's diamond was a fake, then where was *le Coeur Bleu*? Had Jean Philippe hidden it somewhere?

She thought back to the summer of 1940. The Germans had just rolled into Paris and were taking over all aspects of daily life, including the functioning of the police. Jean Philippe was angry at the Germans and furious with the French army and Marshall Pétain for essentially handing over France to its enemies. He told her he had obtained *le*

Coeur Bleu but he never told her anything about helping the Jewish family to escape. She knew now that Jean Philippe had kept the truth from her to protect her.

Her mind raced to the last time she'd seen Jean Philippe. He was going to work, he said, but there was something different in the way he kissed her goodbye. She'd sensed it at the time but hadn't understood it. Perhaps he'd suspected he wasn't ever coming back to her.

Madeleine dissected their last conversation, as she had so many times in the last two years. She'd gone over it and over it, but now she wondered if he had been trying to tell her something. He was so adamant that day...

"Promise me you'll always keep my mother's puzzle box close to you." He took her shoulders in his hands and gave her a gentle shake. "Promise me, Madeleine."

"Of course I'll look after the puzzle box, but I don't understand. The puzzle box belongs to you." Fear suddenly gripped her. "Are you going away? Has something happened? Are you joining the Maquis, *the underground fighting the Germans?"*

"Non, ma chérie." He soothed her with a kiss. "I'm not going anywhere. It's just that these are difficult times. If something were to happen to me, I'd want to know that the puzzle box is safe with you." He fingered her necklace. "Aside from this, it's all I have of my mother."

"Jean Philippe, you're frightening me." Madeleine clung to him. "Promise you'll never leave me. Please don't go away without me."

"I promise I'll always be with you. I'll always be in your heart and you in mine."

He'd kissed her goodbye and left their flat, never to return. The next day, two of Jean Philippe's friends from the police force informed her of his arrest and smuggled her out of Paris, taking her to a safe house in the country. They told her he'd asked them weeks earlier to whisk her out of the city if something should happen to him. He'd protected her, right to the end.

He'd been right about one thing that day. He'd always be a part of her, always own a piece of her heart.

But now she needed to live and to find a way for Hunter to live, as well.

Why had Jean Philippe made such an issue about the puzzle box? She'd always wondered and never understood. Was he afraid that once he was gone she would sell the box? Because of their conversation that day, she had carried the little box in her knapsack to every safe house, every town that was a temporary home in the past two years. She'd kept it close, even though she never found the courage to open the box after Jean Philippe's death.

"You might want to take a very close look at that diamond. The general is trying to stick you with a fake."

"Promise me you'll always keep my mother's puzzle box close to you."

Madeleine sat straight up, her heart in her throat. Could it be?

She threw aside her blanket and got to her feet, feeling her way in the dark to the little wooden table. With shaking hands she lit one of the candles and then brought her knapsack to the table. She pushed aside her few pieces of extra clothing and found the puzzle box, still wrapped securely in the silk scarf inside the larger box. Madeleine held her breath as she removed the puzzle box from its protective layers.

The last time she'd opened the box was two years ago, shortly before Jean Philippe's arrest. He'd patiently taught her how to maneuver the tiny wooden slides in the sequence of moves required to open the box. She'd wanted to give up when the little box refused to open for her, but Jean Philippe wouldn't let her. Looking back, she realized there had been a point to those lessons.

She searched her memory now for that magical sequence of moves. She turned the box over and over in her hands, frantically feeling for the tiny panels that would move and begin the process of revealing its secret compartment. What if she couldn't open the box? Panic seized her.

"I promise I'll always be with you. I'll always be in your heart and you in mine."

With the remembered words in her mind, Madeleine felt a warmth flow through her. Her hands stopped shaking and her heart rate gradually slowed to a normal pace once more. She could feel Jean Philippe's presence beside her, inside her, and the knowledge gave her comfort and strength.

At last her fingers found one of the panels and then another one, and she inched them open. She turned the box over and felt for two more panels that had been loosened by opening the first two. She slid these panels open. And then two more and two more, until the top of the box loosened completely.

Madeleine held her breath as she lifted the lid from the box. The inside of the box was stuffed with a soft cotton cloth that muffled any rattling noises. She pulled the cotton from the box, and her breath caught as she felt a weight inside the cloth. Madeleine set the little bundle on the table and began to peel back the layers, until at last her treasure was revealed. *Le Coeur Bleu* glowed with an eerie blue flame in the candlelight.

A piece of paper folded beneath the diamond caught her eye. She opened the folds and held the paper close to the candle to read. The sight of Jean Philippe's scrawled handwriting brought tears to her eyes.

My darling Madeleine,

If you are reading this letter, I am probably captured or perhaps dead. Please know, my darling, that these months we've spent together have been the happiest of my life. I love you and always will.

The diamond you see here is the famous le Coeur Bleu. *I purchased it from a Jewish refugee desperate to make his escape to England with his family. I got the money to purchase the diamond from my old friend Hunter Smith. Hunter asked no questions. He simply wired me the money. But then the Germans moved into Paris and I had no way of getting the diamond out of France to him. Somehow they became aware that I was in possession of* le Coeur Bleu. *They've been following me for weeks and will likely arrest me. They are angry because I have been helping Jewish refugees from the east obtain false documents so they can reach the non-occupied south of France or even England.*

I have one last trick up my sleeve. The refugee had another blue diamond, not nearly as valuable or famous, but precious in its own right. My hope is that it is good enough to fool the Germans long enough for us to get out of Paris and possibly France.

But if not, remember always that I love you. If you find yourself in trouble, contact Hunter Smith in London. Hunter is the best friend I've ever had, and I trust him with my life. I trust him with your life. He is a good and honest man and will help you if you need him.

All my love,

Jean Philippe

Madeleine held the letter to her heart and wept silently for several minutes. But reality soon took over. She needed to put the diamond back in place before Anne Marie returned.

She quickly rewrapped the diamond and set it back in the puzzle box, returning the lid and gently pushing the sliding pieces back into place until the box once more hid its secret. After carefully rewrapping the puzzle box in the silk scarf and placing it in the protective outer box once more, she shoved it into the bottom of her knapsack along with her few pieces of clothing and her small collection of personal items. Madeleine blew out the candle and felt her way in the dark to her pallet on the dirt floor.

Her heart began to race once more. Now that she had discovered *le Coeur Bleu,* what was she to do with it?

If she and Anne Marie were successful in releasing Hunter, she might never need to reveal anything until she and Hunter were safely in England. But if things went awry, if the tunnel to the wine cellar was blocked, or if they were caught, the fact that she had the real diamond might be used as a bargaining chip.

The idea of handing over the diamond to the Germans, knowing they would use it to tighten their cruel grip on Europe, was repugnant to her. But letting Hunter die was unbearable, unthinkable.

Could she sacrifice her country for the man she loved?

She didn't care if what Natasha had said about Hunter going back for more diamonds was true or not. Even if he was an inveterate thief, she still loved him. But she didn't believe the man she loved was ruled by greed. He'd come to France to carry out Jean Philippe's last wish that *le Coeur Bleu* would escape from Nazi hands. Everything he did, he did out of love.

A few moments later Anne Marie returned, stealing quietly into the root cellar and shutting the door behind her. Madeleine pretended to be asleep as the girl made her way in the dark to her own pallet on the other side of the cellar. Madeleine hated keeping secrets from her, especially after she'd taken her side against Michel and had given her refuge. But Anne Marie was probably safer not knowing that the real diamond rested in Madeleine's knapsack. And if she did know, she'd want to turn it over to the Resistance. She'd never let Madeleine use it to free Hunter, not after what had happened to her sister.

Madeleine spent a restless few hours contemplating the meaning of loyalty before finally falling into a fitful sleep.

Chapter Twelve

Just after midnight, Anne Marie and Madeleine hid their bicycles and Madeleine's knapsack in a ditch and covered them with brush. Crouched behind the thick underbrush in the trees surrounding the chateau, Madeleine felt her heart race with trepidation.

"Remember," Anne Marie whispered, "Monsieur Gagnon says the plane will arrive in the field north of the city at three a.m. The pilot will wait only ten minutes. If you are not there, he will leave without you."

"Yes, I understand." Madeleine's hand shook uncontrollably as she tried to slip on her gloves. Anne Marie gripped her hand, her voice firm and clear.

"It's going to be all right. We can do this."

Even in the faint moonlight, Madeleine could see the conviction on the younger woman's face. She drew a deep breath and nodded. She had to believe their plan could succeed or she wouldn't be able to carry through.

"Are you ready?" Anne Marie asked.

Madeleine closed her eyes and took one last deep, calming breath before nodding. "Yes, I'm ready."

"Good. I probably won't see you again. Once I set the fire, I will get away as quickly as I can. I will leave the bicycles for you and Monsieur Lemay."

Madeleine kissed both her cheeks. "Thank you, Anne Marie. Thank you for everything."

"Good luck, Madeleine. *Adieu.* Go with God."

With that, Anne Marie got to her feet and began skirting the edge of the trees in order to reach the other side of the chateau, where she would start the diversionary fire.

Madeleine prayed silently for her friend's safety and the successful accomplishment of her mission. Then she turned her attention to her own mission.

The door to the kitchen lay just across an open expanse of lawn from her hiding place in the trees. As before, the guards continued to circle the grounds surrounding the chateau in ten-minute intervals. Madeleine waited until a guard had passed before she left the safety of the trees and ran across the lawn to the kitchen door. She sighed with relief when the door opened with a tiny click as she inserted the key. She slipped inside and closed the door soundlessly behind her.

Madeleine negotiated her way through the kitchen in the darkness, feeling along the wall for the broom closet with the hidden panel inside. She stumbled over a bench, banging her knee and muffling a cry, but still she continued on, unwilling to use her flashlight and draw attention to herself.

At last she found the broom closet Collette had marked on her map. Madeleine moved some of the contents, making room to get herself inside to find the secret panel. She ran her hands over the whole back panel of the closet, fingering the edges in search of some sort of latch that would open the compartment. Nothing moved, and she could find no latches or hinges. Panic swelled in her chest, but Madeleine stuffed it down. Hunter needed her.

She leaned against a side wall of the closet, trying to think what to do next. And then she felt it. The wall behind her gave way ever so slightly. Immediately she turned and pushed against the wall. It slowly creaked open. Relief and adrenaline flooded through Madeleine's veins as she slipped through the opening and closed it behind her. She snapped on her flashlight and began to make her way down a set of stone steps, praying they would lead her to Hunter.

The stairway ended, opening into a tunnel tall enough for her to stand up and wide enough for her to spread her arms without touching the sides. It had been hollowed out of the rock and earth beneath the chateau and was supported by huge wooden beams. She followed the tunnel until it branched off in two directions. Madeleine had no idea which tunnel led to the wine cellars and, for a moment, indecision gripped her. At last she decided to follow the tunnel on the left. She walked and walked, but the tunnel seemed to go on and on without leading anywhere. She turned and ran back, retracing her steps until she was again at the intersection. She took the second tunnel until she came to what appeared to be a dead end. The beam of her flashlight showed a wooden door embedded in a stone wall. Madeleine slowly pulled on the door handle, not knowing what she might find on the other side. To her surprise, the open door revealed a solid wooden wall on the other side.

Her heart plummeted. Had this tunnel been blocked off, as Anne Marie warned it might be?

Madeleine scanned the wooden wall with her flashlight, running her hands over the surface as she searched for something that might indicate an opening. At last her fingers tripped over the smooth edges of an iron latch. She pushed down on the latch, and the wall opened a crack. With trepidation and a racing heart, Madeleine pushed the heavy wall until she was able to fit through the crack. Extinguishing her flashlight, she felt her way along a stone wall, the stones cold and damp beneath her trembling hand. Her way was suddenly blocked by what felt like a wooden shelf. Her breath caught in her throat as she felt the outline of cool, smooth glass against her hand. A wine bottle. Her heart raced.

Someone grabbed her. One strong arm held her firmly around her waist, while another wrapped around her throat. Madeleine could barely breathe, much less escape. Fear flowed like acid through her veins.

"Who are you? What are you doing here?"

She knew that voice, though it was disguised by a harsh whisper. She nearly wept in relief.

"Hunter?"

His body stilled, the arm around her neck immediately loosening. "Maddie? Dear God, Maddie."

Hunter turned her around and pulled her into his arms, holding her tightly. Tears of joy sprang to her eyes at being in his arms again.

"What are you doing here? You're supposed to be in England."

"I couldn't go. Not while you were a prisoner here. We must go quickly before they realize you're gone."

"Yes. Lead the way."

But at that moment the small room was flooded with light as the door to the wine cellar crashed open and several German guards marched in. Madeleine blinked against the brightness. General Dietrich followed the soldiers, his mouth pulled into a tight, angry line and his eyes blazing with fury. Madeleine had never seen him so angry. Hunter pushed her behind him, shielding her with his body.

A tall, elegant brunette strolled in on the arm of a balding man with a paunch. Madeleine knew immediately they must be Natasha and Herr Schmidt.

Natasha smiled at Hunter. "Darling, I see you have company. Are you going to introduce us to your guest?"

"I am very well acquainted with Madame Lemay," Dietrich sneered.

He examined the opening to the secret passageway. He smiled at Madeleine, but it seemed more mockery than amusement. "I see the rats have tunneled their way in here. We'll have to check for more such secrets in the chateau and make sure they are all eliminated. We can't let our guests leave before we want them to, now, can we?"

"Enough of these silly games, General." Herr Schmidt wiped his brow with a starched white handkerchief. "I demand to know where the real *le Coeur Bleu* is located. My expert says the diamond you have presented me with is nothing but an inferior imitation."

"He did say that even with its flaws it would still be quite valuable."

"I am only interested in *le Coeur Bleu*. If you cannot produce it, we have no deal."

Dietrich pulled his pistol from its holster and held it under Hunter's chin.

"Yes, Monsieur Lemay, or Smith, or whatever it is you call yourself, I too would like to know the location of *le Coeur Bleu*. If you wish to live, you'll tell me now."

"I don't know where *le Coeur Bleu* is," Hunter said calmly, looking into Dietrich's cold eyes. "I thought the one you had was real, just like you did. I wouldn't have risked my life for anything other than *le Coeur Bleu*."

"If that's the case, you're of no further use to me."

"No! Wait!" Madeleine screamed. "I know where *le Coeur Bleu* is."

Dietrich turned to face her, still holding his gun on Hunter. "Where is it?"

"I want to make a deal."

"I don't make deals with the *Maquis*." His voice dripped with contempt.

Madeleine grabbed wildly at straws. "Then perhaps Herr Schmidt would be interested in making a deal with me."

"How do I know you really have the stone?" Herr Schmidt asked.

"Because Jean Philippe Bertrand was my husband. He purchased *le Coeur Bleu* from a Jewish refugee in Paris. Along with an imitation." She turned to Dietrich, letting all her hatred and contempt show in her eyes. She had the satisfaction of seeing the shock of her revelation on his face. "The general had him executed."

"When he was arrested, Jean Philippe gave up the second diamond to General Dietrich. But he had already hidden the more valuable stone. I only recently became aware of the location of *le Coeur Bleu* and the existence of the second diamond."

"Times two," Hunter whispered. He stared at her. Madeleine prayed he would trust her.

"I see." Herr Schmidt wiped his brow once more. "And what do you want in return for *le Coeur Bleu?*"

"Safe passage for Monsieur Smith and me from this chateau and from Lille."

"I see no reason why that cannot be arranged. As soon as the diamond is in my hands and I am assured it is authentic, you will be free to go."

Hunter struggled against the general's hold. "Madeleine, you can't just give them the diamond! You know what they're going to do with it."

"I don't care. I'm not going to let you die!"

"How very sweet," Natasha drawled. "Perhaps Madame Bertrand would not be so anxious to save you if she knew you were the one who tipped off the Gestapo about her husband having *le Coeur Bleu*." She turned to Madeleine, a malevolent smile on her face. "When I visited him in jail he insisted I contact Jean Philippe, pretending to be him. I was to tell him Hunter had set up a meeting with a diamond buyer, but really the meeting was with the Gestapo. Hunter told me he was always jealous of Jean Philippe. Jean Philippe could do no wrong. He finally got rid of him once and for all."

"That's a damn lie!" Hunter broke free of the general in his effort to get to Natasha. "I would never betray Jean Philippe!"

One of the guards slammed the butt of his rifle into Hunter's ribs. Madeleine cried out as he fell to the floor. Dietrich grabbed her arm, preventing her from going to him.

"Natasha, enough!" Schmidt snarled. "What are you trying to do? Ruin the deal?" He turned to General Dietrich. "We give Madame Bertrand and Mr. Smith their freedom in exchange for the diamond, or our deal is off."

Madeleine knew from the set of his jaw that Dietrich

didn't like taking orders from the South African.

She also knew there was little chance he would let them live once he had what he wanted, regardless of any promises he made.

It was up to her to save them both.

She couldn't take Schmidt and the others directly to *le Coeur Bleu*; it would be too easy for Dietrich to kill them in the forest where she'd hidden the diamond.

No, their best chance of escape was to stay in the chateau until Anne Marie's diversion had a chance to do its job. In the meantime, she would have to buy them some time with her own diversionary measures.

"On your feet," Dietrich roared, as Hunter struggled to regain his footing. The general pulled on Madeleine's arm.

"Take us to the diamond and, if you want to live, don't play games."

Madeleine nodded. She had no intention of playing games.

Staying alive was deadly serious.

Chapter Thirteen

Hunter's ribs hurt like hell, making every step up the marble staircase excruciatingly painful. Madeleine walked beside him in silence, her face tense and drawn. Did she believe Natasha's lies? Could she think him capable of turning Jean Philippe over to the Gestapo? His heart plummeted at the thought that they could go to their deaths with Madeleine believing he'd betrayed her husband, his best friend.

"Where are we going?" General Dietrich demanded. "How much farther?"

"Not much more," Madeleine replied.

"Do you mean to tell me you hid the diamond here in one of the bedrooms on the third floor?"

Madeleine gave him an icy stare. "Sometimes the best hiding places are in plain sight."

They had just reached the third floor landing when an explosion rocked the chateau. Paintings fell from the walls, and the sound of a great deal of glass breaking instantaneously followed. A moment later another deafening explosion shook the building again, knocking them off their feet. Down the hall, part of the roof collapsed. Pain seared through Hunter's body as he landed hard on his damaged ribs, but he saw the general fall, too, as though in slow motion, hitting his head against the hard edge of the top stair. Was he dead? Unconscious? He didn't move, at least. Herr Schmidt, still on the stairs when the second blast hit, had lost his balance and gone backward, head over heels, down the marble steps, taking Natasha with him. The air was filled with dust, and Hunter also caught the scent of smoke.

"Fire! Fire!"

Excited German voices shouted orders and screamed warnings. Madeleine, already on her feet again, grabbed his hand.

"Come," she urged.

As she pulled him along a corridor, Hunter labored to keep up with her. His ribs screamed in protest and his eyes streamed with tears from the dust and smoke, but he kept moving, knowing it was their only chance.

"Halt! Halt!" guards screamed behind them. Hunter could hear their boots slapping against the wooden floor.

"In here." Madeleine tugged him into a bedroom and closed the door behind them. She ran to the bookcases lining one wall of the room and, after a moment of fumbling, opened a secret door.

"Quickly! Go through!"

She pushed him through the small opening and then came through herself, closing the bookcase behind her. A moment later a small beam of light from the flashlight in Madeleine's hand illuminated their tunnel. They were at the top of a flight of stairs. The flashlight revealed wooden walls and steep winding steps. Hunter took a deep breath. At least the air wasn't as smoky in here.

"Can you manage the stairs?"

Hunter didn't care if he had to crawl out of this chateau on his hands and knees. "I'll manage."

"We have to hurry. That fire is much stronger than I expected. I had no idea Anne Marie planned to set an explosion."

Hunter negotiated the stairs as quickly as he could. He'd be damned if he slowed Madeleine down or prevented her escape because of some cracked ribs.

They made it to the bottom of the stairs and hurried some distance through a narrow passageway. Finally, another panel loomed ahead in the flashlight's beam.

"This opens to the ballroom on the second floor. From

here, I'm hoping we can head down the back stairs and out of the chateau."

She opened the small door and slipped through. Hunter followed closely behind her. They were in a small alcove off the main ballroom, a place where guests would have left their coats back in the days of the grand balls held here. Madeleine was helping him to his feet when an older woman appeared around the corner. When she saw them she gasped, nearly dropping the lantern she carried.

"Madeleine! Monsieur Lemay! What are you doing here?"

"Madame Beauchamp." Madeleine took the older woman's hand. "We need to get out of the chateau. Can you help us?"

Although Madeleine seemed to trust the woman, Hunter wasn't so sure. Would her loyalties lie with her employers, the Germans, or with her fellow countrymen?

"The fire is getting closer to this part of the chateau. We must hurry," Madame Beauchamp said.

"What do we do?"

"We go back the way you just came. I know of a tunnel that will take us directly to the stables."

Madeleine nodded. "Quickly. We must hurry. You lead the way, madame."

All three pushed through the panel in the wall once more, and Madeleine put the panel back in place while Madame Beauchamp lit her small lantern.

"This way," she commanded.

They followed her down another set of winding stairs until they reached a second tunnel, this one carved out of the earth and rock beneath the chateau. They followed it to where another tunnel branched off to the left. Madame Beauchamp pointed in its direction.

"That one goes to the kitchen and then eventually to the wine cellar."

"Yes, that is where I came in. I got lost for a time before

I turned around and found my way to the wine cellar. How do you know these tunnels so well?"

"I grew up here," the older woman said. Hunter saw her sad smile in the dim lantern light. "My mother and father both worked here. As a child I explored all the tunnels and secret passageways. I've always loved the chateau, but I believe its time is at an end now."

Madeleine touched her arm. "I'm so sorry, madame."

Madame Beauchamp covered Madeleine's hand with her own. "The future of France and her people is more important than the chateau. But I will miss her."

They walked for what seemed like miles to Hunter. Breathing became more difficult with each step he took. He gratefully leaned on Madeleine when she put his arm around her small shoulders. But he wouldn't give up. He and Madeleine deserved to have a life together.

If she'd have him.

Finally, they came to the end of the tunnel. A ladder leading to a trap door in the roof stood propped against the earthen wall. Madame Beauchamp pointed upward.

"The stables are directly above us," she whispered. "I'll go up the ladder and make sure there are no Germans about, and then I will signal you."

Hunter felt Madeleine stiffen at his side. "Madame, perhaps I should go first. It is too dangerous for you."

Hunter wasn't yet ready to trust Madame Beauchamp. If she wasn't the loyal Frenchwoman she claimed to be, she could emerge from the trap door and signal to the Germans that he and Madeleine were in the tunnels.

"Yes, madame. Why don't you let us go first?"

The older woman chuckled. "Madeleine, I am not so old as to fall from the ladder and break my neck. And Monsieur Lemay, I merely worked for the Nazis. I did not become one. I have no intention of betraying you to them."

He didn't have much choice. With the state of his ribs, he doubted he could push open the trap door anyway. And he didn't like the idea of Madeleine going first, with the possibility of a German soldier waiting for her on the other side with a gun. He nodded, and Madame Beauchamp climbed the ladder and shoved open the trap door. A shower of straw fell around her as the door opened, but all was silent as she pulled herself up through the door and disappeared.

Hunter held his breath as he waited for the woman to reappear. A moment later, she stuck her head through the trap door.

"There's no one here. You can come up."

Madeleine climbed nimbly up the ladder and hoisted herself through the trap door, then turned and stuck her head back through the opening.

"Do you need a hand?"

Hunter touched his sore ribs. "I'll make it."

He climbed up the ladder without too much difficulty, but when it came to hauling himself through the trap door in the ceiling of the tunnel, a feat which required him to use his arms to pull himself up and through the aperture, his resolve nearly broke. Excruciating pain radiated up his right side and down through his arms, making him almost lose his grip and fall back into the tunnel. Madeleine and Madame Beauchamp grabbed his arms, his belt, and then his legs, pulling mightily to haul him over the edge. Hunter lay panting and weak on the straw floor of the stable for a few minutes as he caught his breath and waited for the pain to subside. Madeleine gently rubbed his shoulder.

"I'm sorry, Hunter, but we need to move. Let us help you to your feet."

Hunter was too weak to argue with her. Both women pulled him upright, the pain in his chest screaming.

Madeleine then turned to Madame Beauchamp.

"Thank you so much. We're so grateful for your help."

"You are welcome, my dear." Tears filled her eyes. "*Bonne chance*, Madeleine."

"*Bonne chance*, madame."

The two women embraced before Madame Beauchamp hurried out of the stable and into the night. Madeleine put her arm around Hunter's waist and looked up at him.

"Let's get out of here. The bicycles are hidden a short distance away."

Hunter nodded, but inside he cringed. The mere thought of riding a bicycle over miles of bumpy dirt roads made sweat break out on his brow, but his thoughts were interrupted by a woman's scream as it pierced the silence of the empty stable. A figure engulfed in flames ran in through the wide open door, her cries of pain and terror chilling Hunter to the bone. She fell just inside the entrance to the stable, and Madeleine took off on a run toward her, grabbing a horse blanket as she went. Hunter followed as quickly as he could. By the time he reached the woman, Madeleine had already extinguished the fire on the woman's body, but the damage had been done. Her skin was a charred wreck, her clothing and hair completely burned away. Her face no longer appeared human. She opened her eyes and looked directly at him.

"Hunter. Where is the diamond? We need to get out of here with the diamond."

Bile rose in his throat. "Natasha?"

"Not much time." She coughed, the spasms shaking her body. "The Germans are coming. Where is the diamond? I need it."

"Don't worry, Natasha. The diamond is safe. The Germans can't get it."

Something resembling a smile twisted her ruined lips. The eyes closed. "Good. That's good."

With one last rattling gasp, she was gone. Hunter stared at the barely human form on the stable floor and could feel only pity for a wasted life. Madeleine covered her face with the horse blanket.

"We have to get out of here, Hunter."

Hunter nodded. She put her arm around his waist, and

he leaned on her as they left the stable and slipped quietly through the woods. In the distance the fire at the chateau raged out of control. The sounds of people shouting and sirens blaring filled the night. A thick blanket of smoke hung over the woods.

Madeleine led Hunter to the spot where she and Anne Marie had hidden the bicycles. She pulled away the branches and retrieved her knapsack from its hiding place, slinging it across her back in one elegant motion, and then hauled one bicycle upright and set it in front of Hunter.

"I'm sorry to make you do this, but there's really no other way. A plane is waiting for us." She sounded as if his pain hurt her as much as it did him. The thought gave him hope.

"I know. I'll be fine."

Madeleine took his hand and kissed his palm. A shaft of desire flew straight from his hand to his loins. The timing was all wrong, but he needed to tell her how he felt, how he wanted to spend his life with her, loving her. He touched her face.

"Madeleine, I—"

"Isn't this a cozy scene?" General Dietrich aimed his Luger at the middle of Madeleine's chest. "Monsieur and Madame Lemay sharing an intimate moment. It's really too bad you will have no more moments to share."

Chapter Fourteen

Madeleine gripped Hunter's hand, her heart pounding in fear. They'd been so close to escape.

Dietrich's bloodied face twisted in anger. "Where is the diamond? Give it to me right now, or I swear I'll kill you where you stand."

Hunter squeezed Madeleine's hand in silent communication of support. "She doesn't know where the real diamond is. She was simply trying to buy time."

"In that case I have no further use for you."

Dietrich switched his aim to Hunter. Madeleine stepped in front of him.

"No! I *have* the diamond. I'll give it to you. Just let us go."

"Let me see the diamond first."

Madeleine removed her knapsack and rummaged in the bottom until her fingers felt the edges of the protective box, keeping her eyes on Dietrich the whole time. She pulled the box from the knapsack and held it out to him.

"Here. Take it."

"I want to see the diamond. Open it." When she hesitated, he screamed at her. "Now! *Schnell!*

Madeleine fumbled with the box, her fingers clumsy and as cold as ice. She removed the puzzle box from the outer box and then began moving the slides. After some missteps, the top of the puzzle box opened, and she peeled back the layers of cotton to reveal *le Coeur Bleu*. Beside her she heard Hunter's soft intake of breath. She turned to look into his face and saw his disbelief, his utter incredulity. In that brief look she also saw the accusation in his eyes. Her heart cried at the thought that he believed she'd known of the existence of the second diamond all this time and had kept it from him, risking his life needlessly. She held out the diamond to Dietrich.

"Here. Take it. It's yours. Just let us go."

The diamond glowed blue fire in the moonlight.

Dietrich stepped forward and grabbed it from her outstretched hand, then stepped back, keeping his gun trained on them.

"It's been a pleasure doing business with you. Too bad it is for the last time."

He was going to kill them. If they were going to die, she wanted Hunter to know how she felt. She took his hand.

"I love you," she whispered.

Madeleine closed her eyes and clung to Hunter, waiting for the shot that would kill them both. He put a protective arm around her.

A blast shattered the air, followed by a heavy thud. Madeleine opened her eyes, confused. Dietrich lay dead on the ground, and Anne Marie stood a short distance away, a rifle in her hands. She pointed the gun at Dietrich's body and fired again, her face a mask of hatred.

"That was for Collette."

Tears sprang into Madeleine's eyes, a combination of her grief for Collette and the relief at still being alive.

"You must leave quickly," Anne Marie said. "If the guards heard the shots they may come to investigate. Take the diamond with you. It only causes misery here."

Madeleine wiped her eyes and embraced Anne Marie. "Thank you. *Bonne chance, m'amie.*"

"*Bonne chance.*"

Madeleine hauled the second bicycle from its hiding place while Hunter took the diamond from Dietrich's lifeless hand and placed it back in its sanctuary in the puzzle box. He gathered up the knapsack and handed it wordlessly to her before getting on his bicycle and peddling away. Madeleine took one last look back at Anne Marie and followed him, the box again safely stowed.

****

Hunter's lungs screamed in pain, his ribs burning. Many times he thought he couldn't go on, couldn't pedal one more inch. But despite the pain he pressed on, because he knew if he stopped Madeleine would stop, as well. No matter the cost to him, he had to get her to safety.

By the time they arrived at the rendezvous point, the pilot was preparing to leave. Hunter gratefully dismounted the bicycle, taking a moment to catch his breath and to say a prayer of thanks. After hiding the bikes in a ditch, Madeleine helped him into the small plane. As she placed the seatbelt around his waist, their eyes met briefly. Shock, relief, and fear all flickered in her blue eyes. But she said nothing, leaving him to speculate on her true feelings as she found a sliver of floor to sit on next to his seat, there being only the one in the rear cockpit.

The noise inside the cabin made conversation impossible. Once they were airborne, Hunter closed his eyes and tried to concentrate on something besides the pain. Why had Madeleine never told him of the existence of a second stone? Had she known all along that the stone was in the puzzle box? Did she not trust him enough to tell him? Had she believed all along that he'd betrayed Jean Philippe?

Yet she'd whispered she loved him. Did she truly mean it, or had she said it out of fear, because she thought she was about to die?

The questions swirled in his head. He wanted answers but was afraid to know the truth. He wanted to touch her but was unsure if his touch would be welcomed. If she truly believed he was capable of betraying his best friend and causing his death, how could they ever have a future together?

The idea that Madeleine would no longer be part of his life hurt far more than a few cracked and broken ribs.

****

As soon as they landed at Tangmere Air Base in Sussex, Hunter was taken to the infirmary to have his ribs looked at. Madeleine wanted to go with him, to be by his side and hold his hand while they examined him and bandaged him up. But he didn't ask her to accompany him, and she was afraid to simply tag along. They hadn't spoken since she offered to give up *le Coeur Bleu* to General Dietrich. Did he believe she'd known all along about the diamond in the puzzle box?

The thought made her sick. How she wished she'd opened that damned box two years ago. Then Hunter wouldn't have had to risk his life to retrieve a diamond they now knew was a poor substitute.

She was taken to the women's barracks, where she was allowed to bathe and given some clean clothes. She tried to nap before the debriefing with Special Operations Executive head Alastair Campbell, scheduled that evening. But every time she closed her eyes she saw the disappointment in Hunter's eyes as she strapped him into the seat of the plane, and sleep wouldn't come.

Later, after a light supper, she prepared for the meeting. Monsieur Campbell had travelled from London especially to see them. Madeleine felt at a distinct disadvantage here at the English base, having no knowledge of the language. Luckily, a young female radio operator who knew French was assigned as her translator. When that young woman wasn't with her, others communicated with Madeleine by using a combination of gestures and hand signals that would have been amusing had she been in the mood to laugh.

Her translator wouldn't be allowed into the debriefing session, but she walked her to the office where Monsieur Campbell and Hunter were waiting for her. Campbell extended his hand to her.

"*Bonsoir,* Madame Bertrand."

Madeleine took his hand. "*Bonsoir*, Monsieur Campbell."

He said something else in English that Madeleine didn't understand. She turned to Hunter for translation. He looked more comfortable, as if he were not in as much pain. He was wearing clean borrowed clothing, his hair combed neatly and his face clean-shaven. He looked more handsome than she'd ever seen him.

"He said he's sorry he doesn't speak French. I'll have to act as your translator."

Madeleine nodded. If she was to stay in England for some time, perhaps the duration of the war, she would need to learn English. The thought that she couldn't go home, maybe could never go home again, caused a lump to rise in her throat. She turned her face away, not wanting Hunter to see her distress.

Monsieur Campbell began to speak again. Hunter translated.

"He wants us to tell him what happened, from the time I landed in France until our return here."

Hunter began talking in English. Madeleine made out the occasional word: chateau, Monsieur Gagnon, General Dietrich. At one point Monsieur Campbell looked at her and nodded. Madeleine touched Hunter's arm.

"What did you say to him?"

"I told him how the general was harassing you and I had to pretend to be your long-lost husband. I told him we were forced to live together."

"I see."

As she looked into his eyes, Madeleine remembered making love to Hunter and waking in his arms. Had it been only a little over twenty-four hours ago? She wanted nothing more than to wake in his arms every morning for the rest of her life.

Hunter turned back to Campbell, and she watched his face as he spoke. Such a strong profile, with a straight nose, beautifully formed lips and a determined chin. She could watch him speak all day, even though she didn't understand a word he said.

He turned to her. "I was telling Monsieur Campbell about our first attempt to retrieve the diamond from the chateau."

Madeleine nodded. She remembered how, when they arrived back at her cottage, he had tenderly dried her hair and removed her wet clothing. And then they'd made love. She closed her eyes, reliving the overwhelmingly sweet memory of Hunter's touch, the feel of his body next to hers, the feel of him inside her. Would she ever experience such rapture again?

Hunter continued his debriefing and then turned to Madeleine. "I'm telling him how I was captured trying to take the diamond from General Dietrich's safe, and how Herr Schmidt and Natasha showed up."

"Did you tell him how Natasha blew your cover as Monsieur Lemay and told everyone you were the son of the former American ambassador to France?"

Hunter stared at her in surprise. "How did you know that?"

"I was under the window, hiding in the bushes. I heard everything. I heard you say you thought the general's diamond was not *le Coeur Bleu*. I began to wonder, if the general's diamond was a fake, where was the real diamond? Later, I remembered how adamant Jean Philippe had been that I take care of his mother's puzzle box. That's when I found the diamond. I swear I didn't know before that moment that there was another diamond, or I never would have let you put your life in danger. Please believe me."

"I believe you. I thought you didn't trust me."

She touched his face. "*Non, chéri*. I trust you with my life."

He lowered his gaze. "Then you must have heard Natasha say that I got caught by the police in London going back for more diamonds, but I told you the truth when I said I was trying to put them back."

"I believe you."

"It was Natasha who sent the telegram to JP. She was trying to get her hands on the diamond, but the telegram was intercepted by the Nazis, probably because they suspected him of helping Jewish refugees and were watching him."

Madeleine closed her eyes. It finally made sense. The last piece of the puzzle.

"I know I'm not perfect like Jean Philippe—"

"Perfect?" Tears streamed down her cheeks. "Jean Philippe was not perfect. He was a very good man, but he had faults and foibles like anyone else. Just like you."

Hunter stared into her eyes. He shook his head. "No, I'm not like him. I lie, I've stolen—"

"You risked your life for your principles and for the people you love. You're courageous, and brave, and incredibly gentle, and loving." She smiled. "Isn't it true that even the best diamond can have a flaw?"

"Maddie, I swear to you that Natasha lied when she said I betrayed Jean Philippe. I would sooner have died than betray him."

Madeleine took his hand in hers and brought it to her mouth for a kiss. "I know, *chéri.* I believe you."

"I love you, Maddie. I want to spend the rest of my life with you."

She could barely speak through her tears. Tears of joy. "I love you, too."

Hunter reached for her, pulling her into his lap and kissing her with a passion that gave Madeleine wings. Her heart soared with happiness.

"Ah-hem."

Monsieur Campbell was watching them with an amused expression. Madeleine scrambled from Hunter's lap, giving him a shy smile. Then she dipped her head to Campbell.

"*Je regrette*, monsieur."

But she wasn't really sorry. She was alive, and so was the man she loved.

Hunter and Madeleine finished their debriefing, telling Monsieur Campbell about their escape from the chateau, the diversion created by Anne Marie, and the deaths of General Dietrich, Natasha and Herr Schmidt. He nodded at the conclusion of their story and said something to Hunter, who turned to Madeleine.

"He says the only thing now is to decide what to do with the diamond. He says that since I purchased it, legally it belongs to me. What do you think?"

"I think it should be returned to the refugee who sold it to Jean Philippe. Perhaps that would satisfy the curse of *le Coeur Bleu.*"

"Don't tell me you believe in the curse."

"*Absolument.* Did the people who caused Jean Philippe's death not die horrible, painful deaths just as the curse said they would? But I especially believe it's a good luck charm. It brought us together, didn't it? The diamond may not be flawless, but I believe it is magical."

Hunter kissed her hand, his eyes dancing. "I believe in magic, too."

A word about the author...

Jana Richards has always loved history and is particularly fascinated by the tragic and remarkable stories of the Second World War. The courage, daring, and resourcefulness of the French Resistance inspired her to write *Flawless*, while the tales of love lost and found during the war moved her to craft *Flawless* as a love story.

Jana lives her own love story in western Canada with her husband Warren, her two daughters, a dog named Lou, and three as yet unnamed goldfish.

You can reach Jana at
www.janarichards.net